"MR. WINDSOR!"

Tiffany Martin advanced toward the desk, head held high. Then she placed both palms squarely on the polished mahogany and leaned over until she was only inches away from his startled gaze.

"Well?" he demanded harshly, not budging an inch.

"I have several things to say to you, Mr. Windsor. First, I haven't sold any information and I'd be willing to swear Barry didn't, either. Second, I'm not going home and—I'm not quitting."

He rose, a glint of something—was it amazement or amusement—in the dark eyes. "You surprise me, Tiffany. I wish we had more time to talk now, but I'm booked for the rest of the day. I'll call you tomorrow as I promised."

"I'll expect to hear from you, because I'm not leaving Windsor Enterprises until I've convinced you that my stepbrother is innocent." She stepped back, her stance daring him to defy her.

Amusement definitely had the edge now—betrayed by the slight curve of the full lower lip. "And you'll do anything to prove it?"

"Anything!" she agreed, wondering as she left the room why his eyes were gleaming so brightly.

IRRESISTIBLE LOVE

Elaine Anne McAvoy

Serenade/Serenata
BOOKS
of the Zondervan Publishing House
Grand Rapids, Michigan

Serenade/Serenata is an imprint of
The Zondervan Publishing House
1415 Lake Drive, S.E.
Grand Rapids, MI 49506

ISBN 0-310-46612-1

Edited by Anne Severance
Designed by Kim Koning

Printed in the United States of America

85 86 87 88 89 90 / 10 9 8 7 6 5 4 3 2 1

*In memory of Lucy McAvoy Gilbert
whose Christian integrity has been a
treasured legacy to her many children
and grandchildren*

CHAPTER 1

TIFFANY MARTIN SLIPPED a disk into her small personal computer and brought up yesterday's work on the square, green-tinted screen before her. She felt a glow of pride as she scanned her latest research report on the uses of solar energy.

It had been only three months since she'd started working for Windsor Enterprises, and she still had a hard time believing she was paid so well for doing work she loved. Brushing back a lock of shining, champagne-blond hair, she smiled her thanks as Pam Wilson slid a mug of hot tea onto her work table.

"Slow down, Tiff," said the young receptionist. "It makes me feel guilty to see you starting work before eight-thirty."

Tiffany reached for the steaming cup with one hand as she swiveled her chair around. "No reason to. You're supposed to be taking it easy after that long illness, Pam," she pointed out. "Oh, that!" Pam dismissed her appendectomy with a careless wave of her hand. "I'm all well now. Don't treat me like an invalid." Shifting the subject, she seated herself precariously on the edge of Tiffany's table and crossed her legs, her short, blond curls shimmering against the round, young face. "Wow, do you ever look great today! Isn't that a new dress?"

Tiffany leaned back in her chair, nodding as she took a sip of the fragrant, spicy orange tea. Self-consciously she smoothed down the skirt of the apple green knit dress she'd bought the evening before, glancing around the outer office with its subdued, elegant furnishings. "I thought I needed something a little more sophisticated than the blazers and skirts I wore as a librarian."

"On you, even a burlap bag would look great." There was a trace of envy in Pam's voice as she began applying scarlet polish to her long nails. "Really, it's not fair for anyone to have all your curves *and* the long, slender legs and face of a model."

"Enough!" laughed Tiffany, embarrassed as always when someone mentioned her looks in such glowing terms. Since her early teens, when her slender girlish figure had filled out into the lush curves most women only dream of having, she had been subjected to a steady barrage of comments. Barry, the stepbrother she had loved so dearly, had comforted her, reminding her there *were* men who valued inner beauty. "What's on the schedule today?" she asked hurriedly, to banish the rush of sadness the thought of Barry always brought.

"Nothing special. When's your report due?"

"Next month. This is just the rough draft I'm working on now. Didn't you say Mr. Windsor should be back soon?" Van Windsor, the mysterious owner

8

of Windsor Enterprises, had been away on business since she had come to work. Everyone praised him so lavishly she was dying to meet him. "Isn't he in Pakistan?"

"No, last time he called in, he was in Rio de Janeiro." Pam sighed expressively. "What a life that man leads. Glamour! Big cars! Exotic travel! Beautiful women!"

Tiffany was about to object to the girl's unabashed worship of status symbols when Pam suddenly leaped from the table, almost upsetting the slender bottle of nail polish. "Van . . . you're back!" she squealed, rushing across the room as the double front doors swung open.

Tiffany swirled in her chair, staring at the tall man entering the room. His jet-black hair and charcoal dark eyes created an instant and intense masculine impact. Her first impression was of his self-confident stride, the proud tilt of his jawline, and the casual acceptance of Pam's homage as the most natural action in the world.

When the receptionist hurried around her desk and reached him, he lifted her from the floor with an easy grace, holding her out and away from him. He smiled tolerantly as if he found her flushed young face and the soft fair hair faintly amusing.

Tiffany was intrigued by this first sight of her employer. She took her time, studying him as he set Pam back down on the thickly carpeted floor and began asking questions. She found her eyes drawn to his mobile mouth as he talked, noting its full, frankly passionate look, remembering her stepbrother's mentioning that women found Van irresistible. Her heart

9

began beating a little faster and she forced her gaze lower.

Continuing her intense scrutiny, she stared at the deep cleft in his firm chin. Combined with the rock jaw, it suggested a determination that left her feeling uncomfortable. Her eyes traveled down his beige raw-silk suit, skimming across the broad shoulders to the long legs encased in razor-sharp creased slim trousers. His polished brown leather loafers gleamed under the bright florescent lights.

Without warning Van turned swiftly, his eyes locking with hers, showing total awareness of her interest in him. Embarrassed to be caught staring, she nodded, attempting to smile. With no returning friendliness he strode purposefully across the room and stopped in front of her.

"Tiffany Martin?" Spoken brusquely, her name sounded like an accusation.

In a daze Tiffany stood, facing him with a show of self-confidence that was far more aggressive than anything she was feeling. At such close quarters she noted his face was shadowed with weariness, but his tense, compact body was making no such admission of weakness. His dark eyes raked her contemptuously, dismissing her with an insulting look that matched the tilt of his arrogant head.

She met his glance with a level gaze and spoke firmly. "Yes?"

"It's time we had a talk. In my office." Turning to Joss Collins, his second-in-command, who had followed him into the office carrying a briefcase in each hand, Van asked, "Any reason I can't schedule a conference with Miss Martin now, Joss? I'd like to get it over with."

Shorter by a head than Van and several years older, Joss looked as startled as Tiffany by Van's request. His ruddy complexion flushing a deeper red, he glanced away quickly. "You didn't mention wanting to see Tiff right off. I've already made you a couple of appointments before lunch. The arrangements have all been made . . ."

"Set it for two then." Van interrupted Joss's stammering attempts to bridge the awkward moment. He started for the door leading to the main hallway without waiting to see if the time was convenient with Tiffany.

Joss started forward jerkily, but Tiffany laid a detaining hand on his jacket sleeve. "Is Mr. Windsor upset with my work?" she asked, a slight waver in her voice the only sign she was seething over her employer's officious manner. Joss would level with her. He was the one who had offered her Barry's job after his tragic accident.

Joss shifted his weight nervously onto his other foot, his blue eyes avoiding hers, his voice little more than a murmur. "Don't ask me what's bothering Van, Tiff. I was as surprised as you by that scene. I'll see if I can find out and let you know. For now, try to forget what happened and don't mention this to anyone." He cut his eyes back toward Pam to include her in his warning.

Pam shrugged. "See no evil, hear no evil, speak no evil . . . that's me, Joss."

"Yeah!" he said dryly and both Tiffany and Pam laughed, releasing some of the tension of the moment.

When Tiffany sat down in front of her computer once more, she tried following Joss's advice. Within minutes she gave up, realizing that Van Windsor was

11

not a man who could be banished by a simple act of will. She had recognized a blatant male arrogance in him immediately . . . that physical glow and sensuality that combines with the sense of power arising from the enjoyment of being in command of others. If he made a habit of treating her this way, she'd give thirty days' notice and return to her hometown of Woodville, Texas, she decided.

Glancing over at Pam, she saw the girl efficiently juggling the busy switchboard and queries from several male visitors who had entered the office. Tiffany took this opportunity to slip away, heading for the women's lounge to grab a few moments of privacy.

The tastefully decorated outer lounging area was empty, and Tiffany sank down gratefully on one of the soft French provincial sofas to begin sorting out what could have gone wrong. Hadn't she prayed before accepting this job? If only she'd had the benefit of her stepbrother's advice . . .

But of course she hadn't. This was Barry's job she had taken over. No one could understand how his car had veered off the road that night, turning over and bursting into flames. Barry died instantly, the doctor had assured her later, but that fact was small comfort. Only the pastor's reminder that Barry was in the presence of the Lord and had released his earthly burdens took away some of the pain of his loss. Tiffany brushed back a tear that threatened to slide down her cheek.

No, she had to believe that this was the place God intended her to be. Take Louise Baker, for instance. Louise was Van's personal secretary and, since Tiffany had starting working at Windsor Enterprises,

Louise had come to know and love the Lord. Wasn't that reason enough to believe she was here for a purpose? Tiffany reminded herself. What if Van Windsor was a wealthy, arrogant male who thought he had the right to forget all the common courtesies when dealing with a lowly employee? It would take more than that to make her leave behind the new friends and the wonderful church home she had found in Houston.

When she returned to her desk, Pam's pretty face was flushed with excitement. "Joss just ordered a meal to be catered for us by that posh new restaurant on Richmond . . . the one with the red-and-white striped awnings. Van always does something like that for us when he returns from a long trip. Isn't he super?"

"Count me out," said Tiffany crisply. "I have a lunch date with Joe Hammonds."

Pam turned to face her fully, her eyes round, her voice serious. "I wouldn't snub Van if I were you, Tiff. I've never seen him treat anyone like he did you this morning. That isn't like him. Any idea what's wrong?"

Tiffany sighed, sitting down. "None at all, Pam. Maybe he didn't like the scent of my perfume . . . it wasn't exactly a hundred dollars an ounce, you know."

Pam giggled delightedly. "I'm glad you're not worried, Tiff. But take my advice and come to the employee luncheon. If Joe's any kind of friend, he'll understand."

"He'll understand," agreed Tiffany, reaching for the phone and punching out her date's work number.

"I'm the one who's having a hard time understanding."

Joe was a buyer for the furniture department at a large chain of discount stores in Houston. They had met at the singles class at her new church. Their relationship was strictly platonic at this stage, but she enjoyed having such an amiable escort to show her around the huge city.

Several hours later, Tiffany heard a voice in her ear. "Ready for a cup of coffee?"

She glanced up to meet the smile lighting Louise Baker's green eyes, causing the woman's plain face, framed by shortcropped red hair, to appear almost beautiful. Louise was a widow, fifteen years senior to Tiffany's own twenty-four, but there had been a mutual rapport between them from the moment they met.

"More than ready." Tiffany reached for her purse from her bottom desk drawer. "How are things in the oval office this morning?"

Louise grinned at the creative phrase they'd borrowed to describe Van's plush executive suite. "Unusual!" She lowered her voice as they walked down the hall. "Van seems upset about something this morning. I can't imagine what. Even though there have been a few disappointing ventures lately, the company is showing a tremendous profit overall."

Remembering Joss's orders not to mention Van's curt treatment, Tiffany only shrugged, changing the subject as they entered the spotless chrome-and-steel lounge and crossed over to the help-yourself coffee bar. When they had poured their cups and were looking for two empty seats, Dave Allredge, the head accountant, stood. "Come join us, ladies."

After they were seated, he introduced them to a male visitor, adding, "Tiffany, you must have known Van was due back today. I've never seen you looking more alluring. You ought to wear that dress more often."

"Did I just receive a compliment or an insult?" she teased, stirring the cream into her coffee as her luminous brown eyes twinkled under their fringe of dark lashes.

"Definitely a compliment," said the other man, eyeing her appreciatively. "You look exactly like one of Van's women. Are you applying for the position?"

"Never!"

Louise glanced sharply in her direction. "Isn't he still dating Lee Lowry?" she asked Dave.

Lee was a well-known Houston talk-show hostess and Tiffany was reminded again that several people had already pointed out her resemblance to Lee. Perhaps that was the reason for Van's anger. He might think she was deliberately trying to imitate the woman last linked with his name. The mere idea humiliated her, making the coffee taste bitter in her mouth.

"I doubt if she's still in the running." Dave's gravelly voice brushed aside the woman as if she were no more than a pesky fly buzzing around Van. "His outside limit for any woman is six months, and his, uh, relationship with Lee has run longer than that." Dave's gray eyes glistened with appreciation of his boss's prowess with women, sending another surge of irritation through Tiffany. What was there about Van Windsor that made men admire him more than they envied him? Barry had felt the same way.

Joss entered the lounge, striding toward their table,

15

careful to avoid Tiffany's eyes as he pulled over a chair from a nearby table and joined them. "Everyone ready for a great lunch? The bossman said not to spare any expense."

"Generous of him." The sarcastic words slipped out of Tiffany's mouth before she realized it or could think of some way to make amends.

Louise gave her another startled glance. "How did Van's trip turn out, Joss? He seems a little edgy."

"Profitable. Would you expect less? That man amazes me, the way he picks hopeless business propositions and makes a mint of them. Sometimes I think he's the type of person who would make trouble for himself if there weren't any just to see how he could get himself out of it."

Dave nodded his agreement. "Remember that camping trip in Kenya? I don't have any doubt he enjoyed it when our land rover broke down in the middle of nowhere." Turning to Tiffany, he added, "We had to beg the villagers for a little food. Sometimes I think Van staged the whole thing."

"I wouldn't put it past him," agreed Joss affably. "He likes to see how his people react under pressure. Once, when I went flying with him, he landed his plane in the middle of a desert in Arizona, claiming we were out of gas. Even said he'd forgotten the water jug. I'm telling you, my heart was pounding like a bongo drum."

"That's cruel!" exclaimed Tiffany. "And a little childish, too."

Louise's eyes widened and she shook her head warningly at Tiffany.

Joss leaned back in his chair before saying, "No, Tiff, Van could never be called childish. He can be a little heartless, though, when he thinks it's called for."

"On the basis of a snap judgment?" she persisted stubbornly, still recalling the harshness of her employer's voice when he spoke to her.

Joss's answer was slow and measured as he eyed her speculatively. "No . . . at least he never has before. Don't underestimate him, Tiff. He has a lot more to him than that playboy front he presents to the world. You know, he inherited his wealth. He wouldn't have to work another day in his life if he didn't want to."

"Then why does he?"

Joss lowered his voice. "A need for accomplishment, I'd say. He likes to take risks, tear down barriers, achieve the impossible. He likes to tackle jobs that others wanted to do but were afraid to try. For most of his thirty-one years, he's been an habitual troubleshooter."

"Not with women," returned Dave with a knowing leer. "Van always picks the submissive type."

Joss pushed back his chair, giving Tiffany a piercing glance. "I'd like to meet the woman who wouldn't submit to his every wish."

Tiffany stared back defiantly, her eyes saying: *You're looking at one, Joss.*

The catered luncheon was served in the building's largest conference room and went on for hours, or so it seemed to Tiffany. The others chatted happily, relishing crisp, cold shrimp cocktails, tender tournedos of beef, and braised asparagus. She slid back her chair, picking at her food, determined to stay out of range of Van's compelling gaze.

17

Trying to be fair, she admitted that he seemed genuinely interested in his employees. Leaning forward, he questioned them in turn about their families and activities. The tales of his own adventures were told with brevity and wit, holding the rapt attention of his admiring audience.

The tension Tiffany had been feeling since her earlier encounter with him slowly drained away. Perhaps he didn't understand something in her last report and only wanted to question her about it more thoroughly. Why go looking for trouble until she knew what had upset him?

When the table was cleared by the white-jacketed waiters sent by the catering firm, Van turned his attention to Tiffany. "Don't you agree, Tiffany?" he asked.

"Agree? I'm sorry . . . I–I must have missed something, Mr. Windsor," she admitted, flushing furiously.

"The name is Van and I'm aware you've been completely ignoring all of us," he said softly. The eyes that were fixed on her face narrowed slightly.

As Tiffany started to voice a protest, Louise spoke. "Give Tiff a break, Van. Most women are tongue-tied in your presence the first time they meet you." Her teasing words brought a ripple of laughter from around the table that included everyone except Van and Tiffany.

"You'd make a great diplomat, Louise," he said tersely. Pushing back his chair and standing up, he signaled the caterers to wheel around the dessert cart. "Sorry I have to leave now, but I want the rest of you to enjoy the rest of your meal. I've asked Louise to distribute a little gift to the ladies. It's my way of

18

saying thanks for the way you've carried on your duties in my absence. And . . . for each of you there will be a bonus in your next paycheck."

There were murmured thanks and exclamations of delight as they caught the gleam of gold chains. Nothing in the world could have compelled Tiffany to reach for one, though, and she slipped out of the room the moment Van disappeared.

Rather than return to her desk, she went back to the ladies room, staying as long as she dared, brushing her hair and applying lipgloss until Louise joined her.

"Here you are!" called her friend. "I saved a beautiful chain for you. It's a thick rope that will look marvelous with your turquoise sweater."

Tiffany flinched inwardly as Louise slipped the chain into her handbag. If only she could explain about Van's rudeness to her, but she couldn't let Joss down.

"Thanks for rescuing me in there. I was woolgathering and had tuned everyone out for several minutes."

"Who are you kidding?" Louise sank down on one of the stools before the mirror. "Go on, admit it. Van is one handsome devil."

"Amen to *devil*," she snapped.

Louise laughed. "Dave's friend was right about you. You look exactly like the women Van always dates. I think he was intrigued by the fact that you ignored him. Several times I caught him studying you with more than a little gleam in his eye."

"Sizing me up?" As an opponent? For some absurd reason, she realized, that was exactly what Van considered her.

Louise combed through her short red hair, nodding

vigorously. "Exactly. He's definitely interested in you."

"Well, I definitely do not return the compliment." Tiffany swung her bag over her shoulder to leave.

With the lightest of touches Louise detained her. "Don't antagonize him, Tiff. Those remarks you made in the lounge this morning weren't like you. Don't you know the walls have ears?"

"I know."

Louise was one of Van's most ardent admirers, and Tiffany had no desire to disillusion her. Louise's husband had died several years earlier after a prolonged illness, and she frequently mentioned how helpful Van had been during the dark hours.

The next half hour passed painfully slowly as Tiffany tried to concentrate, dreading the command appearance before her employer. She racked her brain to come up with some reason why he might be unhappy with her work, but drew a blank. As the time neared, she fiddled with some papers on her desk, relieved when the moment finally came so she could end the suspense.

When she reached Louise's office, directly in front of Van's, the older woman seemed surprised to see her. "You say you're supposed to meet with Van at two? I don't have any record of it." She scanned her appointment book with a frown.

"Two," repeated Tiffany firmly, not trusting herself to say more for fear she might blurt out the whole story.

Louise lifted one eyebrow. "I'll check to see if he's ready." She spoke briefly into the phone. "You may go in now, Tiffany."

Tiffany's heart was pounding thunderously as she

pushed open the heavy door. Van was standing with his back toward her, gazing out a large window framing a copper-tinted glass building that was a mirror image of their own. He turned around slowly, surveying her silently for several moments before speaking. "Sit down, Tiffany."

His voice held such a caressing, vibrant quality that she started—feeling almost as if he had touched her. She sat down, grateful for her leather purse which gave her something to occupy her tense fingers.

Van had loosened his tie and unbuttoned the collar of his crisp white shirt, but the casual gesture did not detract from the first impression of impeccable good taste.

He walked over to the massive leather chair behind his desk and sat down, his eyes sweeping her with a disconcerting chill. "As I'm sure you're aware, your work is excellent." The unexpected words of praise were in total contrast to his suddenly icy tone.

She returned his gaze with one equally as intent. "That's nice to hear. Thank you."

"Were you and your stepbrother close?"

Barry! Never for one moment had she thought Van might want to discuss her stepbrother. "Yes, we were. Exceptionally close. I was only six when my mother married his dad, and I literally idolized him. When our parents died within months of each other, he was the only family I had left."

The pupils of Van's eyes darkened in what almost appeared to be anger. "How touching! Are you trying to tell me he was the one who led you into a life of crime?"

Tiffany's apprehension was replaced by indignation. "I suggest you tell me what you mean by that, Mr. Windsor!"

He leaned back in his chair, studying her with a sardonic expression. "This isn't turning out at all the way I expected. I thought you'd try a few tears on me. I'm a real sucker for a beautiful woman who sobs."

Her teeth clamped together in rage, she started to rise, but Van shot forward in his chair, motioning with his hand. "I advise you to remain seated. I'm not finished with this conference—not until I find out who is purchasing information about my business affairs from you!"

Tiffany felt almost sick from shock. She sank back down in the chair, staring at him, numb and speechless.

He continued, "If you needed money after Barry's death, you should have told me." His stormy expression cancelled out any offer of help.

She cleared her throat noisily. "I don't need money. Would you explain exactly what you're accusing me of doing?"

He swirled his chair away so he was facing the window. "Why play games, blondie? I know what you and Barry have done, so denying it only wastes time for both of us. If you're worried about what legal action I intend to take. . . ."

"Stop!" she ordered, furious that he had turned his back to her. "I demand you tell me the basis for your wild accusations."

He turned back to face her. "Lower your voice, please. I'd rather Louise not be involved in this."

Tiffany took a deep steadying breath before continuing quietly. "What are you claiming my stepbrother was doing?"

22

He closed his eyes briefly. "I find this very difficult. Why are you forcing me to bring charges against a dead man?"

Her voice rose shrilly. "So that's what happened! You called Barry in and questioned his integrity. Was that what upset him so much he didn't see where he was going that night?"

"I did no such thing." Van ground out the words. "Shortly after your brother came to work for me, I lost out on several business deals because some of my competitors knew all the details in advance. At first, I had no idea who was responsible. Although everything pointed to Barry, I had no proof. I never mentioned it to him. His death took me as much by surprise as it did everyone who knew him. Immediately afterward, the leaks stopped."

"That isn't proof."

"No, I still managed to keep an open mind although the evidence seemed fairly conclusive. I would never have brought it up again except that the leaks started again last month."

Tiffany straightened her shoulders, breathing a long sigh of relief, and shaking her blond hair so it swirled over her shoulders. "Then that proves Barry was innocent."

He quirked one eyebrow. "Really? All it proves is that his glamorous stepsister took his place. Why don't you be a good little girl and confess who's buying the information. In return, I promise to let you off lightly."

Tiffany felt such a burst of anger she was afraid she might explode. What could she do to clear Barry's name? "You don't have any witnesses," she managed, then realized her very words sounded incriminating.

"Clever girl," he said sarcastically. "I can't make you confess but I *was* hoping you had some conscience. Enough to make you agree to helping me out now that I've exposed your little operation."

"I'm innocent and so is Barry." Her head throbbed with her need to make him believe what she was saying.

Van's jaw tightened. "If you intend to stick to that story, there's nothing I can do about it." He stood, towering over her. "You're fired. Please gather up your things and leave. I'll see that a check is issued for your severance pay."

She rose, glaring back at him. "I have every intention of leaving."

"For once we're in agreement. If you don't mind, I'd appreciate it if you wouldn't mention this to any of the other employees."

"Not mention it?" Her voice rose once more. "I'm supposed to walk out in the middle of an afternoon without a word to my friends? That leaves you a clear field to tell all kinds of lies about Barry and me."

"How much money will it take to buy your silence?" The contempt in his voice swept over her like an ice storm.

"Money!" She spoke softly as she shook her head. "Someone needs to teach you that money is not the answer to everything, Mr. Windsor." She started for the door.

A second later she felt her waist gripped by punishing fingers that turned her around. Fighting down an unfamiliar wave of trembling, she marveled at the power this man had to make her so intensely aware she was a woman.

"You're not leaving here until we come to some kind of understanding," he said. "I don't intend having my employees know I hired a couple of traitors. If money isn't what you're after, then what will it take?"

She stared into the stormy eyes, stunned by the realization that even now, after all he'd said, she still found him attractive. Licking her lips nervously, she whispered, "I won't say anything today."

His eyes flickered in triumph before he stepped back. "Good. Why don't you plead a sick headache today? Tomorrow's Saturday. I'll call you at your home. I'm sure we can work something out then."

She feared she might be sick as she pulled away from him, nodding dully. "What shall I tell Louise? She'll want to know what this conference was about."

"To review your work," he said curtly, returning to his desk with a nod of dismissal. She heard him picking up the phone as she closed the door. Already, it appeared, he had put the unfortunate episode behind him and had moved on to other more pressing matters.

Louise's eyes were bright with curiosity as Tiffany passed her desk. "Got time to run down to the lobby for a Coke?"

Tiffany managed a bright smile. "Not now. I have to . . . gather up some research material." She hated the position Van had put her in; lying was foreign to her nature.

"Oh?" Louise sounded disappointed. "But Van always piles the work on when he first gets back from one of his extended trips. Call me later if you have time for a break."

Tiffany agreed without thinking. Pam was just as curious when she reached her desk and began furtively gathering up her few personal possessions. "What did Van have to say?" the young girl asked.

Tiffany shrugged. "Work." Another lie. Suddenly something snapped inside her. Her work was important to her. It always had been since the year at the university when, as a library science major, she had been encouraged to specialize. Science had always interested her, so she had chosen it as her primary field, which had led to a special project in solar energy. This, however, was the first time she had had an opportunity to apply the knowledge she had gleaned. Since coming to Windsor, she had spent long hours researching the subject. And not even Van Windsor himself was going to prevent her from completing the report!

Slinging down the sack holding her family pictures, she whirled and stalked down the hallway, head held high. When she reached Louise's desk, she swept past her, saying, "I forgot something."

"But . . . wait . . . Van's . . ." The sound of the secretary's voice died off as Tiffany pushed open the heavy door once more and marched in.

Van was sitting sideways, his chiseled profile as remote and inscrutably handsome as ever, speaking into the phone. Out of the corner of his eye he caught a glimpse of Tiffany and began frowning.

She advanced toward the desk, head held high. He glared at her, speaking into the phone, "Sorry, but I've just been interrupted. Talk to you later."

She placed the palms of her hands squarely on the

polished mahogany and leaned over until she was only inches away from his startled gaze.

"Well?" he demanded harshly, not budging an inch.

"I have several things to say to you, Mr. Windsor. First, I haven't sold any information and I'd be willing to swear that Barry didn't, either. Second, I'm not going home and I'm not quitting."

He rose, a glint of something—was it amazement or amusement?—in the dark eyes. "You surprise me, Tiffany. I wish we had more time to talk now, but I'm booked for the rest of the day. I'll call you tomorrow as I promised."

"I'll expect to hear from you, because I'm not leaving Windsor Enterprises until I've convinced you that my stepbrother was innocent." She stepped back, her stance daring him to defy her.

Amusement definitely had the edge now—betrayed by the slight curve of the full lower lip. "And you'll do anything to prove it?"

"Anything!" she agreed, wondering as she left the room why his eyes were gleaming so brightly.

CHAPTER 2

VAN WATCHED TIFFANY as she hurried across the room and closed the door firmly behind her. So she wasn't the guilty party. A variety of emotions swept through him; first, relief, then amusement over her fierce manner and lastly, an intense desire to hold her in his arms. His eyes narrowed and he stared out the window pensively. How long had it been since he'd been knocked sideways by a woman the way Tiffany Martin was affecting him? Next thing he knew he'd be writing love poems to her the way he had to his ninth-grade English teacher.

Chuckling over the strange path his mind was taking, he strode out into the hall. Louise gave him a worried glance, "I'm sorry Tiffany barged in that way. She went by me so fast . . ."

"I was expecting her. How about writing down her address and phone number for me?"

Amused, he watched as Louise struggled to conceal

her surprise. "How have things been going with you, Lou?" he asked.

The red-haired woman lifted shining green eyes toward him. "Van, the most wonderful thing has happened and I have Tiffany to thank. She showed me how to commit my life to Christ, and now everything's turned around. I'm no longer bitter over Jim's death."

Tiffany? A religious nut? It seemed almost unbelievable. Women that glamorous were usually too self-centered to concentrate on anything but themselves. He'd never expected Louise to sound like a fanatic, but if it was helping her get over her grief, what did it matter? Personally, he'd always considered religion to be something you turned to for comfort in your old age.

"That's great," he said awkwardly. "Who's my next appointment?"

Van thanked his secretary for the slip of paper where she'd written down Tiffany's address and phone number and returned to his office. It was several hours later before he finished with his last appointment for the day.

He stood looking out over the twinkling lights of the Houston skyline and found his thoughts drawn once more to Tiffany Martin. The memory of her pale blond hair, the unexpectedly rich chocolate of those luminous eyes, and her soft, seductive voice floated through his mind, permeating the air in the room like the fragrance of a rare perfume. What was there about her that demanded his attention, captivated his thoughts, set his pulses racing? He had difficulty concentrating on his work all afternoon.

The doors to his office swung open and Joss entered

the room. "All finished? Who's the lucky lady tonight, Van?"

"No one."

"That's a switch! Or was there someone special in Rio who's left you immune to anyone else?"

"Hardly. I'm just anxious to get home. Did you let Mrs. Duncan know I'm back in town?"

"I called her earlier, but maybe I'd better tell her you're not going out this evening. Anything special you want her to prepare for your dinner?"

"No," replied Van in clipped tones. "Whatever she decides will be fine. I'm not too hungry." After Joss completed the call, Van said abruptly, "Why haven't you ever married, Joss?"

"Too smart, I guess. Or maybe the *ladies* have all been too smart." His flippant tones made it obvious he thought Van was merely making conversation.

Van sank down in the chair behind his desk and began fingering the slip of paper with Tiffany's name on it. "Tell me more about Tiffany Martin."

Joss shrugged lightly. "She's Barry Nelson's stepsister. He once mentioned that she had the same training he did, so after his death I called and asked her if she'd be interested in taking over his old job."

"I know all that. Has she ever married?"

"Tiff?" Joss laughed sarcastically. "Not on your life. She gives every man around here the frostbitten treatment. I did hear Pam teasing her about some guy named Joe who calls here for her. How was your conference? Is her work satisfactory?"

A sardonic half-smile flitted across Van's face, revealing that he was aware Joss was engaging in a fishing expedition. Although he seldom kept anything concerning the business from his second-in-command, he said only, "Extremely satisfactory."

Van's limousine was waiting at the entrance to the building when the two men emerged a short time later. After wishing Joss good night, Van climbed into the luxurious black vehicle and leaned back with his eyes closed during the short drive home. When he alighted, the doorman on duty in front of the elegant high-rise condominium stepped forward, smiling. "Good evening, Mr. Windsor. Wonderful to see you, sir."

Van attempted a smile but it froze as he remembered Tiffany's words. Did he have anyone in his life who really cared for him or were they all like this doorman, always expecting large tips and gifts in exchange for his friendly greetings? The thought depressed him as he crossed the marble-floored lobby and entered the elevator, pressing the button for the top floor.

When the arched doorways leading into his penthouse apartment slid open silently, Van strode down the hall until he reached the solarium, his favorite room. As he viewed the other rooms, the stark, modern design of his luxurious apartment suddenly struck him as vastly lonely. Even his favorite modern art sculpture added a jarring note. Had it always been this cold and lifeless?

He should have invited friends or some woman over for dinner, he told himself. The long, lonely evening stretched out endlessly before him and he called out impatiently. "Anyone home? Mrs. Duncan?"

"Here, Mr. Windsor. Good to see you, sir." A stolid woman of plain appearance, his housekeeper showed no trace of servility but seemed more like a robot than a warm human being. "Dinner will be ready shortly."

"No hurry. I'll have a drink and unwind first." Van entered the glass-domed solarium that was filled with plants and rattan furniture. Stripping off his tie and jacket, he placed them on the back of the batik-printed upholstered sofa. He unbuttoned the top button of his shirt. He turned to the well-stocked bar, filled a glass with ice cubes, and added a splash of amber liquid.

Sinking down on the couch, he nursed his drink thoughtfully, finding the taste curiously unpalatable. What was his problem tonight? Returning home was something he always enjoyed. For several days he had been anticipating it with a keen pleasure. Now, everything was flat and he longed, instead, for something warm and homey.

Homey? He almost laughed aloud at the very thought. He'd never known a homelike atmosphere in his life. Even Gram's rambling old house in Brenham where he'd grown up had been cold and formal, and he'd never minded it before.

He made a decision and immediately felt better. Tomorrow he'd have Tiffany in for dinner. With a sigh he leaned back into the soft, plump cushions on the sofa, closing his eyes. With any luck at all, he'd probably be listening to her soft, lilting voice at this very time tomorrow. Better than that, she'd be responding to him in a way that would blot out all of these strange feelings of melancholy that were assailing him tonight.

Not wanting to be quizzed about what had gone on between Van and herself, Tiffany avoided Louise for the rest of the afternoon after leaving Van's office for the second time. Promptly at five, she gathered up several folders so she could continue her work over the weekend, vowing that Van Windsor was going to be so impressed with her work that he would never have any excuse to fire her!

She had reached the parking lot before Louise caught up with her. "Tiff, have I ever got something to tell you!" the older woman said. "How about coming home with me for a bite to eat?"

Tiffany rebelled inwardly. She had planned to spend some time alone, sorting out what had happened with Van. "That's too much work for you. Maybe we both need to take it easy tonight. I'll give you a call tomorrow about getting together."

"Well, suit yourself. I did have a few questions to ask you about some verses I read this morning . . ." The hurt which crept suddenly into Louise's eyes made Tiffany feel ashamed of herself.

"On second thought, it sounds like a wonderful idea. Let's eat out and then go over to your place. I've been dying to go to that new Mexican restaurant Pam recommended. She says it has marvelous *fajitas*."

Louise's plain features were transformed by a smile. "Let's ride in my car. I don't trust that wreck of yours."

Tiffany feigned anger. "How dare you talk about 'Charlie' that way?" She was accustomed to being teased about her ancient automobile that still ran beautifully.

Their talk was light-hearted as they wended their way through the heavy Friday night traffic. Louise parked in the garage behind the Galleria shopping center and both women got out. "What level is this new restaurant on?" she asked.

"Second. Pam says it overlooks the ice skating arena."

They arrived a little ahead of the rush hour and were led to their seats almost as soon as they walked into the brightly-decorated restaurant. After giving their orders to a waitress dressed in a colorful Mexican yoked dress, Louise leaned over. "Don't you want to hear my news?"

Tiffany grinned, relieved Louise hadn't questioned her about the conference with Van. "Absolutely!"

"You're going to be proud of me." Louise straightened her shoulders. "I got up my nerve and told Van I'm a Christian."

Tiffany's eyes softened with love for her friend. For days she'd been encouraging Louise to tell others about her new-found faith. "That's wonderful. What did he say?"

Louise laughed. "He looked about as uncomfortable as if I'd asked him to marry me."

A gurgle of laughter escaped Tiffany, causing her to choke on the sip of ice water she'd taken.

Louise continued, "But that's only part of my news. After your second visit in my office, Van came out and asked for your home address and phone number." Her eyes twinkled. "Didn't I tell you he's definitely interested in you?"

"I'm sure it's related to work," protested Tiffany weakly. "He said something about checking with me tomorrow."

"Don't be silly. Only one thing about a woman interests Van."

Tiffany felt herself growing hot. "If so, he's wasting

his time. I detest his type." *Really?* taunted a little inner voice. *Then why have you been thinking about him all afternoon?*

"Keep on your toes, honey. While I think the world of Van as a boss, I wouldn't want to see anyone with his experience take advantage of someone as lovely as you. You could really get hurt if you take him the wrong way."

"I have no intention of taking him any way, so don't waste any time worrying on my behalf."

Louise only smiled mysteriously.

After a meal of steak, charcoal-broiled on a stick, accompanied by soft, warm flour tortillas and guacamole salad with creamy cheese-filled refried beans, the two women indulged by ordering a delicious caramel flan. Over their second cup of coffee, Louise returned to the subject of Van. "I've been thinking, Tiff. Wouldn't it be something if Van became a Christian?"

Before she could stop herself, Tiffany retorted: "And wouldn't it be wonderful if pigs could fly?"

Louise sighed. "I guess you're right. It'll never happen. Van's too self-sufficient to admit he needs anyone—even God."

Consciousness penetrated the blurred dream world as Tiffany lifted heavy lids the next morning, frowning at the sight of her rumpled bed sheets. How long had she slept? With a panicked cry, she leaped up to check the clock. Had she missed Van's phone call?

With a groan she forced herself to sit on the edge of her bed. What was wrong with her? Suddenly her dream resurfaced and she felt heat flooding her cheeks as parts of it came back to her. It had been about Van Windsor, but she couldn't remember what he had been doing—something about begging her forgiveness.

A tiny laugh escaped her throat. "That'll be the day, Tiff," she muttered aloud, yawning delicately and stretching. From the little she'd seen of Van, she already knew the last thing he'd do would be to admit he wasn't in total control of everything.

After showering and eating a light breakfast of orange juice and toast, she padded around the small apartment. Today, all the bravado she'd mustered the day before for her scene with Van had evaporated and now she dreaded talking to him. How had she thought she was going to convince him that she and Barry were innocent?

There seemed to be no answer so she decided to work off her nervous energy. Housecleaning! That should keep her so busy she wouldn't have time to worry.

Tiffany dragged out the vacuum and a basket filled with cleaning supplies. As she snapped on the rug attachment, she surveyed her small apartment lovingly. All the furnishings were from secondhand stores in Houston, but she'd made dusky rose and olive green slipcovers for the sofa and chosen a matching rose spread and drapes for the adjoining bedroom.

The rooms were bright and alive, and the pillows strewn casually on the sofa, along with the baskets overflowing with leafy plants gave them a relaxed, comfortable air that dulled the ache she still felt when she recalled the cheerful home where she'd lived with her parents in Woodville.

She dusted the glass on the framed prints of antique ads for soap powders and long-forgotten brands of foods, and turned her attention to the airy white wicker end tables in the living room. Only the quick determined movements of her deft hands revealed the agitation churning within whenever she remembered Van's arrogant announcement that he would come to her apartment.

By noon the apartment sparkled, but Tiffany's head throbbed with frustration. No phone call. She was the prisoner of her wild dream! With an indignant mutter she took another quick shower to remove the morning's grime and slipped into a pair of jeans and a blue knit top. Hurriedly she left the apartment, choosing to walk rather than take her car to a nearby fast-food restaurant.

The place was jam-packed, not a single empty seat anywhere in sight, so she ordered her hamburger, French fries, and cola to go. On the way home she walked slowly, homesick for Saturdays back home when she'd never been lonely. Most of her friends were married now; several had babies. What was wrong with her? She'd had opportunities for marriage. Was she being too particular, expecting fireworks and explosions when she fell in love?

Still suffering pangs of loneliness when she reached her apartment, she flipped on the TV to a cable station where she could catch the news and settled down on her sofa to unwrap her burger. A bell rang and she had to pause to decide if it was her doorbell or only a noise coming from the TV. With loud, impatient knocking on the front door, she slipped the remains of her meal back in the sack and hurried to answer it.

When she flung open the door, Van was standing there holding a manila folder in one hand. He frowned. "Don't you know to ask who's at your door before you open it?"

Annoyance flashed across Tiffany's smooth features. "I'm from a small town, Mr. Windsor. We always leave our doors unlocked."

His mouth curved into a breath-taking smile. "How about inviting me in?"

Tiffany stepped aside as he entered, her heart beating as erratically as it had the day before when she'd seen him. His large frame filled her apartment. He stood glancing around him with interest. Noticing the sack on her coffee table, he asked, "What's that?"

"A late lunch."

He placed his folder on the table and picked up the sack. "This isn't food. It's flavored cellulose."

"I happen to like it," Tiffany defended. "I'm sure you didn't come here to discuss the nutritional qualities of foods."

He grinned. "Spoken like a true librarian. Don't let me interrupt. Sit back down and finish before your food turns to cardboard."

Tiffany sat down stiffly, thinking of a million rude remarks she could make, all amounting to telling him to mind his own business. Van walked around the room, stopping in front of each poster and scanning it with apparent interest. Her throat constricted and the food threatened to lodge there, but she forced herself to eat every bite.

He took a few books from the shelves and glanced through them and then picked up the large framed photograph of Barry from the top, staring at it intently. At length he turned, "What were you and Barry to each other?"

At his implication her fingers clenched the paper cup, longing to splatter the last of her cola all over his expensive navy plaid sport shirt and the matching solid navy trousers. "We were brother and sister."

He shrugged, setting the picture down. "Just asking. He was your stepbrother, you know." He moved over to the door of her bedroom and studied the contents of the room for several minutes.

Washing down the last bite of her food with the icy drink, Tiffany began gathering up the paper napkins, salt containers, and plastic catsup packets. Once in the kitchen she stuffed them in the trash. When she turned around, Van was standing in the doorway.

"Got any coffee?" he asked.

"Only instant."

"Fine with me," he said, his slight smile infuriating.

Tiffany put the kettle on to boil and spooned coffee into two mugs. When the whistle sounded, she poured the boiling water into each cup, keeping her back turned to Van. Handing him a mug without looking directly at him, she started toward the living room. "Would you please get down to business, Mr. Windsor?"

Van sat down in the overstuffed chair and retrieved his folder. Holding it out, he said, "Here's all the dope on the leaks. This information is top secret. Not even Joss has seen it."

"You trust me?" Her voice was barely above a whisper as all the irritation she'd been feeling toward him melted away.

"Yes, I do."

"You didn't act like it yesterday."

She caught a flash of surprise in the charcoal eyes. "I know. I had to be certain."

"What did I do that convinced you?"

He eyed her over the rim of his mug. "I can't put

39

my finger on it exactly. There's something about you . . ." He stopped abruptly, then added, "I need your help to find out who's the real guilty party."

A shiver of pleasure coursed down Tiffany's spine but she tried to quell it. "I'd like very much to help— to erase the last trace of suspicion from your mind. Barry deserves that much. What can I do to help?"

"Let's start with some basics. What is the nature of Windsor Enterprises?"

She bit her lower lip, feeling like a schoolgirl on examination day. It wasn't easy to explain since the company holdings were extensive and diverse. "Financial dealings. You buy bankrupt companies and resell them. You're also involved in real estate investment trusts and the buying and selling of commodities such as gold and silver."

"What would you say I personally do for a living?" he persisted.

She floundered for an answer.

"Come on now, Tiffany. What's that old counting rhyme? 'Rich man, poor man, beggar man, thief. Doctor, lawyer, merchant, chief.' Will any of those do?"

Her pulses raced as she stared into the dark, compelling gaze. "Rich man, if you can call that an occupation."

"Wrong. I'm going to have to tell you." He leaned toward her. "Basically, I am a gambler, Tiffany."

She swallowed back a hard core of disappointment over his revelation. "You gamble? In Monte Carlo or Las Vegas?"

He laughed. "No. Cards and gambling wheels are for the stupid. I gamble by taking risks—buying companies others have given up on; buying commodities when the price is low and betting that it will go higher.''

When Tiffany only frowned, he continued, ''Do you know the most important part of being a successful gambler?''

''No, I don't. I've never gambled.''

''It's his image. Or the mystique that surrounds him. It's what people believe about him. As long as they're convinced he's a winner, then they react to him with just enough fear and respect to give him the winning edge. But if they begin to view him as a loser, they gain confidence. Do you understand what I'm saying?''

''Why are you telling me this?''

''Because someone is trying to make me look like a loser. As that folder will show you, I've been beaten out on several bids by companies that have definitely had inside information. Look through those papers.''

She glanced through them, not understanding the first few sheets about business deals that had fallen through before she had come to work. Then she became utterly absorbed by what she was reading, letting out a little gasp. ''These last two months . . . the reports I've been working on . . . no wonder, you thought I was involved.''

He nodded grimly. ''And the earlier deals were all researched by your brother.''

''It's all a terrible mistake,'' she murmured, her brown eyes distressed.

''I believe you. I'm sorry I told you about suspecting Barry, but you can see why I was puzzled.''

''Yes, I understand now,'' she said, handing him back the folder. ''Do you have any other suspects?

Anyone at all who might have had access to the information that was leaked?''

"Joss. Louise."

She closed her eyes. "It couldn't possibly be Joss. He's too loyal to you. And Louise?" Tiffany faced him directly, opening her eyes. "She would *never* do such a thing."

He nodded. "That's how I feel. So we're back to square one."

She leaned forward, unthinkingly using his first name, "Van, what are we going to do?"

His slow, seductive smile was like a match lighting dormant passions inside her. Reaching out, he grasped her fingers tenderly, bringing her hand to his lips and brushing a soft kiss on the tingling skin. He spoke softly, "Together we'll think of something, Tiffany."

CHAPTER 3

FOR THE BRIEFEST OF MOMENTS golden lights flickered in Van's eyes, and Tiffany found it almost impossible to breathe. His fingers tightened over her hand as they stared at each other. With enormous effort she turned her head away, breaking the invisible web shimmering between them.

Gently she removed her hand, saying huskily, "I'm glad you're so confident, Mr. Windsor." Her voice was embarrassingly husky and she cleared her throat.

"I like it better when you call me Van," he murmured, leaning away. "Why is it you find my name so difficult to say most of the time?"

"Because you're my employer." Suddenly she began laughing, a light, lilting laugh that banished the lingering air of intimacy.

His eyes narrowed. "What's funny?"

"I was trying to imagine calling my last boss by his first name. I think he would have fainted from the shock."

Van smiled. "Am I anything like him?"

She laughed again. "Not in the least. He was an institution around Woodville and extremely solemn."

"Then let's dispense with him for now." He stretched out his long legs, linking his hands behind his head. "Where shall we have dinner this evening, Tiffany? At a restaurant or at my place?"

Just like that! No thought of asking *if* she'd have dinner with him!

Fuming inwardly, she answered, "I already have a date."

"Break it."

"You must have a low opinion of me."

His glance was bright with amusement. "Don't tell me you've never broken a date before. If so, I'll wager you're the only woman who can say that."

"If I have, I'm ashamed of myself."

"We couldn't allow that," he mocked. "Call your date and tell him you have to work late. It won't be a lie. We'll discuss what we're going to do to ferret out whoever has been trying to throw suspicion on you and Barry."

The idea was tempting. As long as this black cloud hung over her head, she'd be uneasy even though Van had made it plain he believed her. Anyway, Joe wouldn't object to going alone to the singles class country-western barbecue if she told him she needed to work.

On the other hand, she didn't care for Van's arrogant disregard of other people's plans. She shook her head, smiling lightly. "Sorry, but I really can't do that. We can talk for a while longer *now*, though."

Van lowered his lids, dropping his hands to his knees. Something about the downward slope of his shoulders hinted at a vulnerability that surprised her and she experienced a gush of tenderness. His clipped, icy tones when he spoke dispelled that notion quickly, however. "I've already spent hours trying to come up with other suspects. None of the companies that have underbid me have any common link."

"Surely Joss has commented on what's happening."

"During this same period of time, we've had a lot of successes, so he's been too busy to notice that all the leaks have come from yours and Barry's projects. It's only a matter of time, though, before he makes the connection."

Tiffany swallowed hard. "There has to be some clue you're overlooking."

"I'm working on the security angle. You know how carefully those reports are guarded. After you hand them over to Joss, he adds his opinions and gives them to me. I make notations on them, including what I'm planning on bidding and they're sent on to Louise to file in the safe. Only three people know that combination, as far as I know: Joss, Louise, and myself."

Tiffany lifted brown eyes to him. "What I put on those reports is information that's available to anyone."

"I know that."

"Then how could I have ever been implicated? I have no idea what you write on them."

"I'm aware of that. When I suspected you, I thought perhaps Barry had observed Louise's opening the safe and had passed the combination on to you. By the way, we've changed it since you came, but the leaks have continued."

Tiffany shook her head, puzzled. "I can't imagine what's happening. I never discuss my work with anyone."

"Not even casually? To your hairdresser or a male friend?"

"Never."

He grinned at her serious expression. "I'm not trying to accuse you again." Rising, he picked up the folder. "Since I can't convince you to play detective with me this evening, I'll have to work on it myself. Next week we'll get together and see what we can come up with."

"Yes," she agreed, standing to see him out.

When they reached the door, he turned, trailing a finger down her cheek, smiling into her eyes. "See you, Tiff. Have fun tonight."

The sincerity in his voice warmed her. "You, too, Van."

After the door closed behind him, Tiffany wandered through her apartment, stepping out on the small balcony behind her bedroom. Admitting to herself that Van Windsor appealed to her far more than he should, she mentally kicked herself for not accepting his dinner invitation. What would it be like to spend an evening in his company?

He was an extremely attractive man, but she knew that wasn't the only reason she was drawn to him. No, something besides a physical awareness, as strong as that was, had sparked between them and she hoped fervently that she would have a chance to get to know him better. But only as a friend, she reminded herself with an impatient shrug.

She and Van lived in different worlds, with different life styles, different goals, and, much more important, different beliefs. Never would she even consider allowing herself to become romantically involved with someone who didn't have a personal belief in Christ. The gulf between them would be too vast to bridge.

The rest of the weekend seemed anticlimactic after Van's visit. The evening spent with Joe dragged by and she found it tedious to listen to his long stories about his last fishing trip. When he started to kiss her at her apartment door later that evening, she stopped him, telling him in as kindly a manner as possible that she felt nothing but friendship for him. He accepted it with only a slight show of disappointment, but made no mention of another date.

On Sunday she and Louise attended the early morning church service together. The minister's message was one of a continuing series on love and marriage. Tiffany listened intently. She had needed this reminder of how important it was to have a marriage based on more than physical attraction.

On their way out, Louise was eager to discuss it. "I've got the makings for spinach salad and sandwiches at home. How about lunch?"

"Love it, if you're sure it's not too much trouble."

"You know I hate eating alone," said Louise.

Once seated at her small round table in her cheery kitchen, she began discussing her own marriage. "If only I had been a Christian when we were married. I think Jim was, but he had drifted a long way from his childhood faith. Then, when he became ill, I was so bitter against God for allowing that to happen to my husband, I wouldn't even listen when Jim wanted to talk about it."

47

"But you were very ready to hear me talk about God's love and His forgiveness," pointed out Tiffany.

"I was absolutely desperate. Running from God isn't much fun. Thanks, Tiff, for caring enough to share your faith with me."

Tiffany blinked back tears of joy. Why had she ever doubted for even a moment that she was where God wanted her to be?

Louise changed the subject abruptly. "Did Van ever call?"

"No, he didn't." If only she could tell Louise what was happening.

"Good. I can tell you quite frankly that I was concerned yesterday. Last night Joss and I went to a party together and he mentioned it, too."

Tiffany lowered her eyes and concentrated on the fringe of lettuce peeping out from between the thick slices of bread. "Mentioned what?"

"Van's interest in you. Seems I wasn't the only one who caught it. Joss said Van asked him a lot of personal questions about you."

"Probably because I'm the newest employee at Windsor's."

"And by far the most beautiful." Louise took a sip of her iced tea before continuing. "Take the advice of someone much older than you, Tiff. Van is dangerous where women are concerned."

Tiffany laughed lightly. "You make him sound like Attila the Hun."

"He has a low opinion of women for some reason. Joss says the first time he suspects one isn't being totally truthful, he drops her like a hot potato."

"His personal life is really none of my business,"

protested Tiffany, a hard knot twisting the pit of her stomach.

Louise gave a short, disbelieving laugh. "Don't think you can remain immune to his charms. Van has a way of making every woman around him think she's something special."

Tiffany couldn't look directly at Louise as she asked, "Has he ever been married?" There was a brief meaningful pause before Louise replied and Tiffany realized her friend had seen through the casual inquiry.

"No. Don't misunderstand me; I really care for Van. There's nothing I'd like better than to see him happily married to a wonderful girl like you, but I don't want to see you left on his discard heap, either."

Tiffany feigned a shudder. "You do have a way with words, Louise. Thanks for the warning."

"Just call me Mother Louise," teased the older woman.

All day Monday Tiffany had a sense of anticipation, expecting at any moment to see Van walk into the outer office where she sat working. Several times she considered ringing his extension to ask if he'd thought of anything that might help clear Barry's name, but she stopped herself. He knew where she was if he wanted to talk to her.

By Tuesday she began keeping an eye out for him every time she went to the lounge or stopped by Louise's desk to chat for a few minutes. Still no sign of Van.

By Thursday morning she had accepted the fact that he had no intention of seeking her out. Probably he had found her dull and unexciting compared to the glamorous jetset types he had collected. She decided not to think about him.

It almost worked, too, except for all those times when she saw his name on the glass doors or caught a glimpse of the letterhead on the office stationery. Then, when Pam insisted on reading her a blurb from a gossip column reporting he'd been seen with a visiting movie starlet at a supper club, Tiffany found it a little difficult to breathe for several minutes. Aside from that she was doing just fine, thank you.

When the phone on her desk rang at eleven on Friday morning, she answered in her usual manner: "Research Department."

"Did anyone ever tell you your voice is enchanting?" Van spoke huskily and Tiffany felt such a burst of exhilaration she had to hold herself in check.

"Librarians seldom get such effusive compliments."

"Ah, that's because librarians seldom look like candidates for Miss America. That blond shade of your hair is stunning with those big brown eyes."

"I'm glad you approve, since there's not a lot I can do about either." Like everyone else, he must have assumed she had changed her hair coloring. "Was there something you wanted?"

He chuckled softly. "Have I just been told to mind my own business?"

"You're very clever," she said demurely.

"I can't believe it—my first, faint word of praise from you. How about having lunch with me today? I think I've got a solid hunch about a suspect."

"That's wonderful . . ."

"Having lunch with me?"

She laughed. "You're really impossible, you know. What time?"

"Buck will be waiting for you at the main entrance at eleven forty-five."

"Buck?"

"Haven't you seen the short, muscular guy with a crewcut around there? He's my chauffeur, messenger, bodyguard, and all-around good friend."

"I had no idea who he was. Where are you?"

He lowered his voice. "Don't ask questions. If we're going to take this cloak-and-dagger business seriously, we've got to inject a little mystery into it."

She fell in with his light-hearted mood. "Shall I wear dark glasses and a trench coat?"

"No, I prefer that rose silk dress you have on."

Puzzled, she glanced around. "Now I *am* curious. Where are you calling from?"

He began chuckling again. "You haven't been out of my sight much this week, sweetheart."

She felt herself blushing. "Keeping tabs on me?"

His voice dropped. "You know better than that. Don't forget, Tiff. Eleven forty-five in front of the building."

Pam was full of questions as soon as Tiffany replaced the phone. "That was Van, wasn't it? I recognized his voice when he asked for you. What did he want? Is Buck taking you to meet him?"

"Goodness," laughed Tiffany, "I thought receptionists were trained to be discreet."

Pam had come over to her desk. "Come on, Tiff. Tell me what's going on. Did Van *really* ask you out for lunch?"

"He really did," mimicked Tiffany affectionately.

She had a special feeling for Pam, recognizing in the nineteen-year-old a loneliness that can be understood only by another person without family ties and living in a large city.

"Ooh, Tiff. That's fabulous! Wouldn't it be something if Van falls for you? He's so rich!"

"I've been invited to lunch, not marriage," Tiffany pointed out dryly. "Anyway, rich men are no greater than others."

"You'll never convince *me*. I've been poor most of my life, and it's no picnic."

"You look as if you're doing very well now, so it must not have been too terrible." Pam's determined search for a rich husband made her the object of a lot of teasing around the office. Tiffany longed to say something about the girl's false values, but Pam adamantly resisted anything to do with God.

Shortly before time to leave, Tiffany stood and Pam hurried over once more, retying the bow at the neckline of the rose dress and adjusting the gathers in the softly flowing skirt. "You look fantastic. Why don't you put on some of my blusher and eye shadow?"

"Van will have to take me as I usually look," returned Tiffany with a laugh as she reached for her purse. On impulse, before leaving her desk, she took out a key to the bottom drawer and locked away the papers she had completed printing out that morning .

The sleek, black limousine slipped through the heavy traffic with surprising ease. Leaning back in the plush upholstered back seat, she tried willing her racing pulses to be still. This could be heady stuff, she warned herself. If she didn't keep both feet firmly planted on the ground, she might find herself in over her head.

She concentrated on the rows of tall glass buildings that lined both sides of the freeway, making Houston one of the nation's most modern cities. Sometimes though, the fast pace almost overwhelmed her, and she longed for the ambience of the piny woods near her own hometown.

When Buck exited the freeway and turned down Memorial Drive, Tiffany sat up straighter. This was her favorite residential area. While much of Houston lay sprawled on a swampy, flat plain that barely managed to be above sea level, this area of stately homes was surrounded by towering pines and sturdy oak trees. Spanish moss clung to the trees, casting the whole neighborhood into peaceful shadow.

The restaurant where Buck stopped was a quiet, unpretentious place located in a shopping center. Tiffany thanked the driver as he took her arm to assist her from the car, and he nodded politely. His serious expression was almost too much and she had to stifle a laugh as she thought how surprised he'd be to learn this was the first time she'd ever been chauffeured anywhere.

Once inside the small, dimly lit foyer, a maître d' appeared. When she gave her name, he led the way past several small, inviting dining rooms into a secluded alcove. Van rose from a small table covered with a snowy-white cloth. There was something slightly wicked about the smile on his aristocratic features. As the maître d' disappeared from sight, Van reached for her hand, drawing her to him. They stood very close, gazes locking, and it seemed the most natural thing in the world when his lips touched hers in a brief, thrilling kiss.

Tiffany was breathing rapidly as he pulled out her chair and she sank into it. No one, she was absolutely certain, had ever felt such sensations. She stared into his dark, compelling eyes as he seated himself across from her, trying to tell herself he was no different from the other men she had met, but she wasn't in the least convinced.

His eyes raked her approvingly, taking in her pale cloud of soft, silky hair and the wide-set brown eyes, fringed with their thick, dark lashes, that were seriously studying him. No other woman had ever affected him this intensely and he ached with the thought that she was so elusive, so unattainable.

Everyone has a price, he reminded himself cynically. He only needed to find Tiffany's. The trouble was he actually liked her air of honesty and innocence, and he respected her enough that he didn't like to think about manipulating her into something she might regret. The thought made him smile. *Careful, Windsor. This woman's going to prove to be your Waterloo.*

A waiter broke the palpable silence that hung between them, his discreet manner adding to the atmosphere of intimacy. Tiffany felt overwhelmed by the large, leather menu and was grateful when Van said, "They make a great Caesar salad here. How's that for starters?"

Within minutes Tiffany felt comfortable with Van. "This is a lovely restaurant," she told him. "So unpretentious on the outside, but elegant inside."

"You're very elegant on the outside yourself," said

54

Van softly. "But I'd like a glimpse of what's going on inside."

She shrugged. "I'm totally uncomplicated."

"What I see is what I get?" He grinned disarmingly.

"Funny, I don't remember saying that," she countered lightly.

"You seem very practiced at fending off male compliments."

Tiffany hesitated. It would be stupid to pretend she wasn't aware that her brand of looks appealed to many men. On the other hand, she wanted somehow to let Van know that she wasn't flattered by praise for something she had done nothing to earn or deserve. "Barry was a great help in pointing out to me that looks are not all that important in the long run," she said quietly.

Van studied her with his dark head cocked to one side. "Barry was a great guy. I found him unusual in many ways."

Tiffany raised her hand to signal her refusal as the waiter started to pour wine into her glass. "Unusual? In what way?"

"It's hard to say. Just his general demeanor. He always seemed to go the second mile to help everyone. Once, when I quizzed him about it, he said something about being a Christian." Van took a sip of his wine. "Louise tells me you're religious, too."

From his inflection, Tiffany knew his attitude toward Christians was not what she would have wished. "I'm a Christian, if that's what you mean. But that isn't to say I think I'm better than anyone else. Christians are just people who recognize they're not very good, so they need help from God."

"I can't imagine your not being good, Tiff," he teased lightly. "I really admired Barry. That's why I was so surprised when I first noticed the link between him and the leaks in my business."

She leaned forward. "Barry would never have done that, Van. Do you have any clues yet?"

"In a minute." Van turned as the waiter appeared with a cart and deftly began tossing the fresh, crisp greens with a theatrical flourish before cracking a raw egg and adding oil and spices. When he had served generous portions on each of their salad plates and moved away, Van spoke in a low voice. "I have one suspect, Tiffany."

"Is it someone I know?"

"If you've attended any parties with Joss and Louise, you may have met him. His name is Bob Hartman."

She searched her memory. "Tall? Blond? Almost too good-looking to be real?"

Van's eyes narrowed. "So you're not as indifferent to men as I thought."

She laughed at his ill-concealed display of jealousy. "I'm not blind."

Van took his time answering. "Why haven't you ever married? I thought most women wanted nothing more than a domesticated husband with a fat paycheck."

"I find that remark insulting."

His slight laugh was cynical. "Then scratch it and accept my apologies. To get back to Bob. We grew up near each other, with our families running in the same social circles. Both of us attended the same military boarding school and joined the same fraternity in college. Basically we're in the same sort of business

56

now. His father is my real rival, though, because Bob is such a good-time Charlie he's never settled down. For some reason, he's always been intensely envious of me."

"You're too modest," teased Tiffany, tracing patterns on the crystal glass she was holding.

He raised an eyebrow. "Don't tell me I'm about to hear you say something nice about me."

"Not a peep. I wouldn't think of adding to that inflated ego. All these other women beat me to it."

"Rumors, Tiff. It's part of that image I told you I need to spook the competition. I'm really a loner most of the time."

"Mmm . . ." She sounded totally unconvinced and he laughed.

"Now, back to Bob and the case of the missing information. The only clue I have at this point is that silver mine deal that fell through. I believe that was Barry's last report and your first."

She nodded, buttering a chunk of hot French bread. "I remember it well. Joss was very upset when you lost out."

"Bob's father's company underbid me by the magnificent sum of a hundred dollars."

"Couldn't that be a coincidence?"

"As likely as picking three Kentucky Derby winners in a row." He waited until the waiter removed their salad plates and served creamy beef stroganoff on thin ribbons of noodles with a side dish of crisp, steamed broccoli. "No," he continued, "That gut instinct of mine is telling me that Bob Hartman is the one getting hold of the information."

"And selling some of it to other competitors so you can't prove it?"

"Exactly, my dear Watson."

"Then who's selling it to him from our office?"

He expelled his breath harshly. "That's what I don't know. I do have an idea as to how you can help me find out, though. Still willing to help?"

All her burning desire to clear Barry's name shone from her eyes. She repeated her earlier offer. "I'll do anything, Van."

He laid down his fork, picking up one of her hands in his, murmuring, "Thanks. I'd like for you to test my theory that Bob wants everything I have and will stop at nothing to get it."

She frowned, something warning her to pull back, but his fingers tightened on hers. "What do you want me to do?"

His free hand reached up, cupping her face gently, his thumb stroking fiery trails along the soft skin. "We'll have to convince Bob we're lovers."

For one startled moment she could think of nothing to say and then she shoved her chair backward, almost tipping it over in her hasty retreat. "That . . ." she stuttered with outrage, "that is the last thing in the world I would ever agree to, and I can't believe you don't know that!"

He leaned back in his chair with deep frown lines creasing his brow. "You did say *anything*," he reminded, his eyes bright with mockery and something else she didn't want to define. His eyes ran the length of her slender throat, resting on the revealing pulsebeat in its hollow.

She waited, bitterly expecting him to make some remark about hers or Barry's guilt that would place her in a seemingly impossible position. He surprised her, saying instead, "I don't expect you to help me without getting something in return. I'll pay you enough to make it worth your while.''

Her voice quivered with suppressed rage. "Money? Is that the way you solve all your problems, Van? The other day I called you a rich man, but I was wrong. You're so poor . . . poor in everything that really counts.''

Van's mouth tightened. ''That line has a great ring to it, but I haven't found anything or anyone yet who couldn't be bought. The secret is in finding out the price.''

''Then I feel sorry for you.''

''Spare the pity. Name one thing I can't buy.''

She took a deep breath. ''You can't buy God's love. Or eternal life. You see, Van, God can't be bought. He does all the giving. His Son, Jesus Christ, paid the price for us and we only have to accept His gift.''

''All intangibles,'' he said, smiling easily once more. ''I have no argument with what you're saying. But we're dealing with the here and now, not some pie-in-the-sky theory.''

Tiffany sighed with frustration, praying silently for the right words. Van continued, ''How about your offer to help? Are you reneging on that promise?''

''No, I . . .'' The waiter appeared once more with cups of rich, brown, fragrant coffee and she concentrated on stirring a spoonful of heavy cream in hers. ''I can't pretend to be your lover, Van. I can't go against my principles.''

He chuckled softly. ''Then how about going to a party tomorrow night with me and letting Bob think you're dating me? Surely that wouldn't tarnish your lily-white reputation too much, my little saint.''

CHAPTER 4

LOUISE WAS CHATTING with Pam in the outer office when Tiffany returned from lunch. "Tiff, why didn't you tell me you were lunching with Van?"

"I didn't know myself until only minutes before," said Tiffany, searching through her purse longer than was necessary for the keys to her desk to avoid seeing the slight hint of reproof in her friend's eyes. Leave it to Pam to make a big deal of spreading the news all over the office.

"Well?" demanded Pam, almost breathless with curiosity. "Where did you go? Did Van ask you out again?"

Tiffany felt like screaming with irritation. If only Van hadn't insisted that she not tell anyone about his suspicions, she wouldn't be placed in this impossible situation. "We went to a restaurant so exclusive I didn't even see a name out front. The food was fabulous . . ." She glanced around with a sigh of relief as she saw a stranger enter the office. Lately she'd begun regretting that she'd moved Barry's desk out of the office he shared with several men. Pam's curiosity was growing too intense these days.

"Time to get back to work," said Louise, rising decisively, as if suddenly remembering her responsibility to set a good example in front of the young receptionist. "About tomorrow, Tiff." She stopped in front of Tiffany's desk before continuing, "I'll have to cancel our NASA trip. Joss and I have been asked to work overtime, and you know how much I appreciate the extra money. See you at church Sunday."

"No problem," assured Tiffany with a smile. That was good news. On the ride back from the restaurant, she had been wrestling with the problem of getting out of the trip she and Louise had planned. She didn't want to tell Louise about the party she'd agreed to go to with Van. With that worry off her mind, she settled down for an absorbing afternoon of work.

Saturday morning Tiffany slept late, waking only in time to grab a quick bite of breakfast before going next door to care for the neighbors' baby girl so they could go shopping for several hours. As she played with the smiling, cuddly infant, Tiffany mulled over what she should wear that evening. On several occasions Louise had invited her to one of the social events she and Joss frequently attended on Van's behalf. The women guests had all been dressed expensively, in glittering, glamorous creations that must have cost more than Tiffany earned in a month.

She and Louise had enjoyed seeing all the society women, but tonight would be totally different. Van probably created a stir wherever he went. Not only would he be the most attractive man there, but his wealth and self-confident manner must make him one of Houston's most sought-after bachelors. In spite of her determination to keep in mind that Van's interest in her was only on the business level, she felt excitement bubbling inside her. How could any woman resist enjoying an evening as his date?

The bright-eyed baby began squirming uncomfortably and Tiffany carried her into the kitchen. After locating a bottle of orange juice from the refrigerator, she warmed it to room temperature under a stream of hot water. Cradling the warm, soft bundle in her arms securely, she placed the nipple in the eager mouth, smiling as she felt the quick, strong tug. Once settled in the rocker, Tiffany's mind returned to her problem of what to wear that evening.

It would be foolish to go out and try to buy something impressive to wear. On her budget she could never compete. Anyway, she'd feel more comfortable in something familiar. With that thought, she decided on a simple black dress with the string of pearls that had been her mother's and began humming softly as the baby's dark lashes fluttered down on the pudgy cheeks and lay still. Tiffany was almost sorry to relinquish the child to her parents when they returned a short time later.

Van called in the middle of the afternoon, his voice brusque and businesslike. "Glad I caught you in, Tiffany. I tried this morning and this is the first chance I've had since. I've arranged for Buck to pick you up in an hour to take you to Annebelle's. Is that inconvenient?"

Annebelle's? The name sounded faintly familiar. "No, I'm not busy." Her voice trailed off in bewilderment.

"Great. Annebelle has agreed to personally handle this job. She's preselecting several dresses and you're to choose the one you think is best."

What dresses? Suddenly it clicked! She'd read about Annebelle's in the papers. It was an exclusive salon and boutique, catering to the wealthy of Houston by offering beauty treatments, hair designs, and clothing all under one roof.

"I have a dress that should be suitable." Tiffany feared that if she breathed deeply, she might unleash some of the irritation his words had produced. How dare Van assume he could take over in this highhanded manner?

"I'm sure it's more than suitable," he agreed smoothly. "But it's necessary that you be such a standout tonight that everyone present will notice you. I thought I'd explained to you that our suspect operates by wanting what others admire."

"I understand that but I'm not in the habit of accepting clothing from men. From what I've heard, Annebelle charges a small fortune for one of her makeovers."

His laughter rang with sincerity. "If we even get one clue tonight, it'll be more than worth it. Consider this a business expense. By the way, you do realize you'll be receiving standard overtime pay for any hours you spend helping me?"

Tiffany was glad Van couldn't see how furiously she was blushing. Had he thought she was hinting for more pay? Feeling thoroughly helpless to make him understand her point of view, she said, "I should never have brought money into this, Van. I'm afraid you and I are on different wave lengths about that subject."

"So you tell me. Can you make it to Annebelle's? Afterward, Buck will bring you over here and we'll go to the party with some friends."

"As long as you understand that the dress will be returned to you when the party's over. Also, I have the right to refuse to wear it if I don't like anything Annebelle offers."

"Agreed. I'll see you in a little while, Tiff. I've got some more to tell you about Bob. The more I dig into this, the more evidence I'm finding that he's our man." Van spoke quickly, as if he were in a hurry.

"I hope we learn the truth soon." As soon as Tiffany replaced the receiver, she wondered if she were letting herself in for something she'd regret. The important thing to remember, she reminded herself, was that Van viewed all of this as only a necessary part of his business. Didn't the mention of overtime pay prove that?

The sight of the limousine was less intimidating this time and Tiffany felt relaxed as Buck drove her to the River Oaks area of Houston. All of her self-imposed *sang froid* melted at the sight of the imposing entrance to the salon. "I'll be waiting for you when you're finished," said Buck in his usual deferential tone.

How many other women had Van sent here? The thought sent a shiver of distaste down Tiffany's spine, but she held her head high as she entered the reception room. "Tiffany Martin," she told the woman behind the counter.

"Ah, yes. Annebelle's special client. Please. Come this way. Would you like something to eat? To drink?" The softly accented voice of the auburn-haired receptionist fluttered in welcome.

"Nothing, thank you." Tiffany's throat felt as dry as cotton.

There was no need to be told which woman in the room was the famed Annebelle. Tall, slender, dark-haired with a regal air, the woman who stepped forward was absolutely stunning. Her practiced eye traveled scrutinizingly over Tiffany, making her feel like a piece of prime rib in a butcher's shop. "Excellent," she said at last. "Good bones, beautiful hair, and of course, fleshy in all the right places."

"Sounds like I'd be a winner in a dog show," said Tiffany with a slight smile.

Annebelle's coal-black eyes twinkled but her voice was as impersonal and well-modulated as before. "Let me explain our procedures. You'll be taken to the skin care room and given a facial. Then while the pack is doing its magic, you'll have your choice of a massage or the whirlpool. Next will come time with our hair designer, manicurist and make-up artists. Meanwhile I'll be selecting various dresses for you and seeing if any of them meet your approval. Shall we begin?"

"Sounds like a dream," admitted Tiffany.

The next hour was a whirlwind of activity and before long Tiffany was caught up in the pleasure of being totally pampered. She tried not to think of the cost. As Van had pointed out, if it helped to stop the information leaks in his company, it would be worth-while. After her time in the spa, clad in a terry robe, she was waiting for the manicurist when Annebelle returned.

The silvery-voiced woman held up three dresses, explaining the styling details of each. "Do any of these seem right?"

"They're all too . . ." Tiffany stumbled around, searching for a way to make herself understood. At length, she decided the direct approach was the best approach. There was no reason to tiptoe around in such a timid fashion. "Annebelle, I should have explained to you when I arrived. I won't wear anything that's designed to show off more than it hides."

Annebelle laughed lightly. "Pity. You have such delightful curves. Ah, well, I'm certain I can find something to please. While Charles works his magic on your skin, I'll keep looking."

It took several more consultations before Tiffany finally settled on a dress—a frothy midnight blue confection, its bodice of clingy silk with a V-neckline and the skirt a swirly chiffon that billowed out from the snug waistline.

Dressed from the skin out in the expensive garments for which Annebelle's had gained its reputation, Tiffany stared at herself in the three-way mirrors as the hairdresser deftly put his finishing touches on her unfamiliar, wildly curled hair style several hours later. Silvery eyeshadow with smudgy dark blue eyeliner made her eyes seem those of a stranger. Serious doubts about her ability to make it through the long evening settled like a heavy weight.

Annebelle was ecstatic. "You are perfection! But is something wrong? You're not pleased?"

"No . . . everything is just fine."

The older woman's flawless face broke into an unaccustomed smile. "You have been a delight, my dear! So many of my clients are a little . . ." She stopped and then shrugged expressively. "But enough of that. You will be pleased to know that Mr. Windsor called a few minutes ago to check on our progress. I think he is planning some surprise . . . perhaps a little something from his jeweler?"

Tiffany fought back a shudder. What must Annebelle be thinking of her? "Thanks for all you've done," she said feebly. It wasn't Annebelle's fault that she was filled with conflicting emotions.

Tiffany wasn't aware how late it was until she stepped outside the elegant porte-cochere doors of the salon. For a moment she stopped, her eyes adjusting to the late afternoon sun after hours inside Annebelle's flattering pink walls. Buck was holding the door to the limousine, and she wondered who had signaled him she was finished. His eyes gleamed appreciatively. "You look great, ma'am."

Tiffany adjusted her billowing skirt as she slid into the back seat. "I wonder if Cinderella felt as uncomfortable in all her new finery."

"Don't say that. I spent all morning polishing this Rolls, and I don't want it turning to a pumpkin," he returned with a chuckle.

The ride was brief—too brief as far as Tiffany was concerned. Buck turned off the main street, stopping in front of a sleek high-rise condominium consisting of three graceful towers stretching high above a terraced island of greenery. The car slipped under a concrete arch, coming to a halt before a uniformed attendant. Buck swiveled around to speak to Tiffany as the tall man swung open her door.

"I'll call up and let Mr. Windsor know you're on your way. Go inside the lobby and take the elevator to the left. When you get to the top floor, walk straight down the hall to the doors at the end."

"Thanks, Buck." Tiffany slid out, not liking the

scrutiny the doorman was giving her. Ignoring his proffered arm, she entered the lobby and located the elevators. The ride up was over entirely too quickly and, when she stepped out of the elevator, it seemed she was in another world. She stopped in front of the arched doorways at the end of the hall, trying to steady her nervous breathing when the entrance glided open. Van was standing there.

For a moment neither spoke. Tiffany stared at him openly, feeling almost as if he were someone she had never seen before. His elegant dark formal evening clothes, with the ruffled white shirt, set off his tanned features to perfection. He returned her gaze, taking in Annebelle's production with a look that told Tiffany nothing of what he was thinking.

"Trick or treat," she punned weakly, feeling that if he didn't speak soon, she couldn't bear it.

He stared a moment longer and laughed, shaking his head ruefully. "I'm glad you view this as just a costume. Frankly, I like the version I saw yesterday better."

"Me, too. I have this feeling that if I so much as turn my head, something will fall off." She followed his gesture and moved inside the room, aware of his expensive masculine scent as she passed him.

"You'll definitely be the hit of the party tonight," he murmured, slipping his arm around her waist and attempting to draw her closer.

She stepped aside deftly, protesting, "Careful or you'll muss my dress." Glancing down the long hallway, she caught a magnificent view of the lights outlining the skyline of Houston. "How beautiful!"

Van sounded surprised. "You like this place?"

Tiffany stopped and gave the open spaces an

68

appraising look. One large room dominated the area, resembling a Picasso painting with bold geometric lines and splashes of vivid colors from primitive handwoven rugs that broke the stark white of the walls and furniture. Tall trees growing out of chrome tubs and mirrored cubes holding surrealistic lamps and art objects vied for attention. It was too cold, too harsh, she decided. Realizing that Van was waiting for her answer, she said quietly, "I'm afraid my tastes haven't been cultivated to appreciate this much elegance."

"That's no answer," persisted Van.

"If you really want my opinion, I frankly find it too unreal." An involuntary shudder coursed her spine. "Perfect for a museum, but how can you relax here?"

"I don't stay home much. My decorator said this was an exact mirror image of my personality, only she was much more flattering. She described it as bold, urbane, sophisticated." His eyes reflected amusement and she realized this ability to laugh at himself was one of his most appealing traits.

Footsteps sounded down the marble hallway and Tiffany turned. A woman in a black uniform with a white apron approached.

"Mrs. Duncan," said Van. "I'd like you to meet Tiffany Martin."

Mrs. Duncan's clear blue eyes revealed nothing. "My pleasure, Miss Martin. May I bring you something?"

"We'll wait for our other guests," said Van. "Right now I have something to show Tiff." He touched her elbow lightly and steered her down the hall until they stopped at a small, plant-filled room just off the living area. The room was in total darkness except for the twinkling lights from the star-laden sky revealed by the glass-domed ceiling.

"Here's where we can relax," said Van, indicating the sofa. "Was your afternoon tiring?"

"Not in the least. Everything is designed to give you a sensation of floating on clouds. I've never had so much attention in all my life."

He frowned slightly. "You liked it?"

"As a once-in-a-lifetime treat. I couldn't imagine wanting to do that very often. It makes you feel about as useful as a piece of clay an artist is sculpting."

The frown disappeared and a smile spread across the chiseled features. "Wait here."

He returned within moments bearing a velvet box, speaking quickly before Tiffany had time to react. "Here's a necklace for you to wear tonight. All my—"

"—friends will be expecting Van Windsor's date to be wearing something sinfully expensive," she finished in an exasperated voice. No way was she going to let Van make some kind of intimate ceremony out of this. Barely glancing at the intricately carved gold chain with the large diamond pendant, she slipped it around her own neck, treating it as casually as a piece of inexpensive costume jewelry. "Are you sure I need to wear this?" she asked quietly.

Van's dark eyes glittered with amusement. "Quite certain. Remember, Tiff, it's all for a good cause."

She sighed. "I hope so. What was the news you had about Bob?"

Van sat down next to her, making her all too aware of the warmth of his body as he turned toward her, one muscular hand dropping onto her bare shoulder with a light touch that sent electricity tingling through her. His voice was subdued. "A very good friend told me that Bob's firm has begun inquiring into the solar energy consortium that I'm interested in. That means he knows the topic you're researching."

Tiffany's luminous brown eyes widened. "How could he?" she said, her voice shrill with disbelief. "I've never had a conversation with the man."

Van shook his head wearily and leaned back against the soft cushions on the rattan sofa. "I know. It's really a mystery."

An inexplicable urge to reach out and stroke his cheek in comfort assailed her and she struggled to speak in a normal voice, "What should I be watching for this evening?"

"Nothing, really. If Bob approaches you, act a little haughty." He chuckled softly, adding, "As if I need to tell you that."

She smiled ruefully. "What do you hope to gain from tonight?"

"I'm planting seeds," he answered mysteriously. "If any of them sprout, I promise to let you in on what we'll do next."

"Please do. I don't want to make any mistakes."

His eyes flickered softly and he put a finger under her chin, tilting her face. For just a heartbeat, Van studied her upturned face, then his hand dropped, the fingertips brushing down her arm in a caressing trail. "That's wise, Tiff," he said huskily. "You want to be careful not to make mistakes."

She lowered her eyes, breathing unsteadily, certain they were no longer talking about the information leak in his company. Marveling at her deceptively calm tones when her heart was doing jumping jacks, she said, "I hope I don't disappoint you, Van."

Both looked up as chimes sounded softly. Van jumped to his feet, calling out, "I'll get it, Mrs. Duncan."

Tiffany took the few minutes he was gone to steady her breathing and gain control of her reeling senses. She couldn't allow herself to be distracted by Van's attractiveness. She was here on company business tonight, she reminded herself ruthlessly, so she better get the glitter dust out of her eyes and start concentrating.

The sound of footsteps on the long marble hall mingled with laughter. Tiffany straightened her flowing skirts and took a deep breath. She was thankful she had when she glanced toward the door and saw the shocked glances on Louise's and Joss's faces as both came to an abrupt halt.

Van seemed unaware of the drama of the moment. "Have a seat and I'll fix us something to drink. What did you two think of the factory in Baytown?"

Louise's voice sounded strangled. "Tiff . . . what a sur—surprise. You look stunning." She sank into a chair on the opposite side of the room.

Joss was equally ill-at-ease. "I didn't realize Tiffany was your date tonight, Van."

Van handed him a glass filled with an amber liquid. "I did my finest selling job before she'd agree. What would you like, Louise?"

"Nothing," she managed, the look of surprise changing to an icy glare.

"How do you like Van's condo?" Joss asked, sitting down across from Tiffany.

Van's laughter rang out. " 'Cold and ostentatious'— I believe those were her words."

"It does have a breath-taking view of Houston,"

said Tiffany, wondering how to break the barrier that had suddenly been erected between Louise and herself. Inside, she was fuming. Why hadn't Van mentioned the names of his friends?

"Perrier and lime, Tiff?" Van asked.

She nodded, eager to have something to hold in her hand.

Louise suddenly gasped, "That's a beautiful necklace, Tiffany."

Tiffany's eyes flew open and she glanced at Van helplessly. *Say something*, she pleaded silently. *Explain that I'm not taking jewelry from you.*

"It was my mother's," said Van in a low voice. "Tiffany looks lovely in it."

"Yes, yes . . ." Joss was almost too hearty in his approval and Tiffany saw him shoot a hard glance Louise's way as if he knew how shocked she was. "Hope there's something good to eat at that party tonight. Louise and I were running late, so we didn't stop for anything since noon."

"Then I suggest we go check it out," agreed Van. He rose and led the way toward the elevator.

When they reached the ground floor and stepped out into the humid tropical air so typical of spring evenings in Houston, Tiffany stayed close by Van's side, her mind gnawing anxiously at something to say to let Louise know she was mistaken.

A large dark blue sedan was waiting in the curved drive and Tiffany allowed herself to be escorted around the car and helped in by the doorman. Van slid in behind the wheel and she met a searching gaze from warm, dark eyes. She felt his breath fanning her neck as he leaned over, his lips touching her cheek with a gentleness that unnerved her. "You're doing great, Tiff. It'll be over soon," he murmured.

As he started the engine, Louise's voice sounded from the back seat. "Tiffany, when did you get that dress?"

"I went to Annebelle's . . ."

"Ooh . . ." Louise's voice warbled with excitement. "What's it like there? Tell me what happened."

Tiffany sighed and began a condensed version of the afternoon's happenings. Van glanced over at her from time to time, smiling over her attempts to downplay the events. Just as Tiffany finished answering the last of Louise's many questions Van braked to a halt in front of a massive colonial-style home. "Here we are."

Joss was frowning as they got out of the car. "Sounds like a circus," he grumbled. "Wonder what we're letting ourselves in for tonight."

Van seemed preoccupied. "I told you I have an important reason for coming," he said in clipped tones. They made their way around to the back of the house, the noise level increasing with each step they took.

Tiffany stopped in surprise, scarcely believing the sight of a Roman-styled atrium wildly decorated with ostrich plumes and turquoise and pink ribbons. The atrium was large enough to cover an Olympic-sized swimming pool and still leave space on all four sides. The whole scene was reminiscent of a colorful epic movie celebrating a Roman orgy.

From across the crowded area a willowy woman approached, wearing a one-shoulder turquoise chiffon gown with enough jewelry to appear grotesque. Reaching Van's side, she stood on tiptoe to plant a kiss on his cheek. "Now that you're here, darling, the party can begin."

Van returned the kiss lightly. "Have you met Tiffany Martin, Jill?" He turned to Tiffany. "Our hostess, Jill Hopkins."

"Not another one," squealed Jill, giving Tiffany one scathing glance before turning back to concentrate on Van. "You always pick such perfect specimens, it makes me feel all washed out in comparison." Without waiting for a reply, she spotted another arrival and went scurrying off.

"Whew," said Joss. "That woman makes me tired just watching her. Have you located the food yet?"

They staked out their claim on one of the tables and then made their way to a row of purple-clothed tables lining the far side of the atrium. Tiffany forced herself to fill her plate with bite-sized helpings of the caviar-stuffed eggs, pickled artichokes, spicy olives, warm breads, and an assortment of thinly-sliced meats and delicately flavored cheeses.

Determined to keep Louise from asking any more embarrassing questions, Tiffany kept up a steady patter of remarks about the various morsels of delicious-looking food. Somehow she had to get a few moments alone, give herself enough time to think of a way to explain to her friend what had happened tonight. But how could she do it without betraying Van's trust? Trailing behind the others as they wended their way through the crowd, she prayed silently for an answer to her dilemma.

Louise seemed equally determined to find out more. "When did you ask Tiffany to this party?" she asked Van with an engaging grin.

He smiled back. "I've been asking Tiffany out since

I first set eyes on her. You have very good taste in friends, Louise."

"I view her almost as a daughter," said Louise with a piercing glance.

Van laughed loudly. "I think I'm being threatened."

"Drop it," demanded Tiffany. "Lou, you're entirely too young to be my mother." This was becoming more complicated by the minute. Now Louise was in danger of making her boss angry with her.

"Good food," said Joss, with a satisfied groan. "Some of your friends leave me a little cold, Van, but they do know how to put on a good spread."

A shadow fell across Van's shoulder and Tiffany glanced up. She recognized the tall, blond man who was leaning over, smiling in a way that made her skin crawl. Van stood, holding out his hand. "How are you, Bob?"

"Fine." Bob Hartman continued to stare at Tiffany. "Haven't we met somewhere before?"

CHAPTER 5

"BOB HARTMAN, TIFFANY MARTIN," Van introduced smoothly. "Will you join us, Bob?"

Bob pulled out a seat, still studying Tiffany. "Only for a moment. I'm certain I've seen you before, Miss Martin."

She shrugged, spreading a delicate butter and shrimp mixture on a flaky croissant.

"Hello, Bob," said Louise in a determined tone.

He glanced her way, "Hi, Louise. Hi, Joss. Does the boss have you two working again?"

His rudeness made Tiffany boil. Several equally rude remarks swirled through her head, but she bit her tongue, wondering why Van was allowing this with no protest. Suddenly Bob reached out and tapped the diamond pendant she wore. She recoiled angrily. Bob seemed oblivious to her reaction. "Quite a stunner, Tiffany. You must make Van a very happy man."

Tiffany opened her mouth to protest, but Louise

grasped her arm firmly, glaring at Bob. "Will you come to the powder room with me, Tiff?"

After a sharp glance in Van's direction, Tiffany stood and followed Louise through the crowd. "What was that all about?" she asked when they reached the door of a guest house beside the pool and pushed open the door. "Why are we running from Bob?"

"I don't know what's going on here," hissed Louise, "but I don't like it."

"I don't, either," returned Tiffany hotly, tears stinging her eyelids.

The room was empty and Louise whirled around to confront her. "Really, Tiffany, I'm surprised at you. Don't you know what accepting that diamond from Van implies?"

Tiffany shook her head mutely, fighting back the tears.

Louise shoved her in front of the mirror and pointed to the sparkling diamond. "Then I'll tell you. It's an advertisement that you're Van's latest lover. He *always* gives his women a diamond."

"No," gasped Tiffany. She gazed through misty eyes at the sight of herself in the gold-framed mirror. Flushed cheeks. Too much makeup. A dress subtly accentuating her curves. "Lou, you know I'm not involved with Van in the way you're thinking, don't you?"

Louise lowered her eyes. "But . . ."

Tiffany shook her arm. "Look at me. I'm telling you there's nothing like that between Van and myself. You've got to believe me."

"The dress . . . Annebelle's . . ." Louise's hand swept over Tiffany. "Why didn't you mention you

78

were going to this party with Van? I thought we were friends."

Something snapped inside Tiffany and she straightened her shoulders, sparks of fire dancing in her eyes. "Don't worry, Lou. I'm straightening this whole mess out soon." She whirled and hurried out of the room and through the crowd.

Still charged with adrenalin, she stopped in front of Van and demanded, "I'd like to see you alone. Now." From the corner of her eye she saw an attractive woman sitting in the seat she'd just vacated. She realized too late that she was interrupting a conversation between the woman and Van.

He stood to his feet, frowning slightly. "Yes, what is it you want, Tiff?"

For a moment Tiffany's determination wavered but the feel of the hard, cold diamond on her neck was a potent reminder. "I'm sorry to interrupt, but I must see you," she said firmly.

He smiled but there was still a puzzled look in the dark eyes. Turning to the woman who was watching with an amused expression, he said, "You'll have to excuse me now, Lee. Good to see you again."

Lee Lowry. The TV anchorwoman that rumor had it was the last woman in Van's life. Embarrassment flooded Tiffany but she managed a cool smile in Lee's direction as she and Van moved away.

Van led the way with Tiffany close beside him until they reach a darkened area thick with tall trees. He stopped and she moved against one of the trees, leaning against its rough bark as she struggled to catch her breath. "Well?" demanded Van with impatience.

His grating tone was all the spur she needed to remember the anger she was feeling. Reaching up with unsteady fingers, she removed the necklace. "Here. Take this. I can't go through with this any longer."

He made no move to accept the necklace in her hand. "I'd like to know what's happened, Tiff. Try calming down."

"Calm down?" Her voice was shrill with anger. She slapped the diamond against the palm of his hand. "You can quit pretending that you didn't intend for everyone here to think I was your lover—and this diamond was your signal."

His sudden burst of laughter was infuriating. "There's not one word of truth in that. Frankly, I'm not overly fond of diamonds myself and I've never given one to a woman in my life."

Tiffany refused to be placated. "You're saying that Louise was lying?"

He shook his head, slipping the necklace into his pocket before resting both hands on her shoulders. A languid amusement still softened his chiseled features as their gazes meshed. Taking a calming breath, Tiffany tried to ignore his evocative masculine presence as her eyes moved slowly over his face, coming to rest on the firmly molded lips as he began speaking. "Louise has only been listening to some silly gossip. I've already explained to you that there's a public image I've allowed to be circulated because it's been good for business. I was hoping you could see that my private self is entirely different."

"I didn't agree to be part of that image," Tiffany maintained stubbornly but her voice was softer and the anger was dissipating rapidly.

His hands caressed her shoulders gently, easing away the tension. "I'm sorry you feel I've humiliated you, Tiff," he continued. "It's the last thing I'd ever want to do. What can we do to make things right?"

Tiffany felt as if she were in deep water, and didn't know how to swim. Why did she find it so hard to think straight when he was near? Closing her eyes resolutely she forcibly conjured up mental images of the disappointed look on Louise's face as she'd struggled to understand what was happening.

The mental picture cleared Tiffany's mind and she opened her eyes. "We'll have to tell Louise and Joss the truth. Unless you suspect them, I don't understand why you insist on keeping this from them."

Van dropped his hands to his side and stepped back. His voice was tight. "My company is like my family, Tiff. I didn't want to start suspicions, have everyone watching each other to see if they could catch someone in an act of disloyalty. Can you understand that?"

Involuntarily Tiffany reached out and stroked Van's jacket sleeve. "Yes, I can. But I can't be a part of deceiving Louise. I'm sure they'll work with us."

He shrugged. "I hope you're right. Let's find them now and we'll go somewhere so the four of us can talk."

"Thank you, Van. It means a lot to me."

"It better," he answered, tucking her hand into the crook of his arm as they started back.

Joss was talking to a group of men when they found him and seemed relieved to be rescued. "You find Louise," ordered Van. "Tiff and I will express our regrets to the hostess."

"I wonder what that woman you were talking to when I so rudely interrupted is thinking," said

Tiffany, a little later as they were making their way to the area where their car was parked.

Van chuckled. "Lee? I'm sure she was stunned that I obeyed you so docilely." Wrapping an arm around her waist he added, "I'm a little shocked over the way I react around you, too."

Tiffany couldn't suppress a grin. "I'm afraid I erupted like a volcano," she admitted. "You bring out the worst in me."

They were both laughing when they reached the car where Louise and Joss were standing. Louise gave Tiffany a sharp look but was silent as she climbed into the back seat.

"Tiff and I need to talk to you," explained Van as he started the engine. "Does my place sound okay?"

"How about mine?" said Louise. "No offense, but I feel so intimidated in your place I can't talk. There are a few things I think I need to say to you, Van."

Van nodded. "Your place it is, Louise."

"What's all the mystery about?" grumbled Joss good-naturedly. "If you expect me to take part in some serious discussion, you better put a big pot of coffee on."

When they reached Louise's house, she hurried into the kitchen and reached for the coffee pot, ignoring Tiffany's offers to help. Joss and Van pulled out seats and settled in at the round table. When the cups were in front of them, Van was the first to speak. "Tiffany came to the party with me tonight as an employee, the same as you two," he explained slowly. "I've asked her to help me solve a mystery."

Louise's green eyes were round with surprise as she glanced guiltily at her friend. "Why didn't you say anything?"

"I asked her not to," said Van. With an economy of words he ran through the problems that the company had been having, ignoring Joss's angry outbursts over the thought of a traitor in their midst. Van finished, "Once Tiffany convinced me she and Barry were innocent, I knew I'd have to widen my investigation. Do either of you have any clues?"

"But we're your prime suspects," murmured Louise with uncertainty.

"Never in my mind," reassured Van. "It has to be someone with access to privileged information."

"No one has that," said Louise with firmness. "I've never left the safe unlocked or any papers left out."

"You know I never talk," said Joss. "So where does that leave us?"

Van shrugged. "Back at square one."

Louise suddenly shot an appraising look Tiffany's direction. "But I don't understand. How was Tiff's going to the party supposed to help?"

"I'm using her as bait," said Van. "Bob Hartman . . ."

Joss's mouth hardened. "If he had any way of getting information, I'd say he's the criminal. That guy hates you, Van."

"And it was his Dad's company that made that bid," chimed in Louise. "He's the one. I just know it. But how is Tiffany involved?"

Van chuckled. "Bob always goes after the women I date. Did you see he was Lee's escort tonight? If I'm right, he'll be calling Tiff in a few days and asking her out."

"Oh, no, you don't," said Louise firmly. "I'm not

throwing my friend to the wolves. Tiffany is not going out with that no-good playboy."

"I agree, Louise. But she can have lunch with him, talk on the phone a few times, see if she can get any leads as to who is helping him in our company."

"Hey, you two. I don't like being talked about like I'm not here," said Tiffany. "I have every intention of taking part in finding out who's guilty. After all, it appears Bob Hartman has made Barry and me look terrible."

"But who's giving him information?" said Joss with a frown that creased his forehead into deep grooves. "Who does he know at Windsor's?"

"Almost everyone, at least in a casual way. He always manages to show up at most social events where I'm involved," answered Van.

"Dave! Dave Allredge! I heard him say that Bob had invited him to his ranch," inserted Louise.

"I can't believe it of Dave," groaned Van, glancing down at his cup. "Look, I think we've said enough for tonight ... this whole thing worries me half to death." He glanced over at Tiffany. "Finished with your coffee?"

"Yes," she said quickly, filled with sympathy for Van's distress.

"Need a ride to my place to get your car?" Van asked Joss.

Joss shook his head. "Lou can run me over later. I think we'll spend a little time going over the names of all the employees. Hopefully, we'll come up with something."

Van's smile was grim. "Thanks, but don't work at it too hard."

He seemed distant, engrossed in his own thoughts,

as they drove toward Tiffany's apartment. He was still silent as he parked the car, and they made their way up the steps. In an attempt to lighten his mood when they reached the top, she glanced at her watch, saying, "You can tell Buck that my dress didn't turn into rags at midnight."

Van's puzzled look cleared slowly and then he began smiling. "I'm afraid your evening didn't turn out too well. Sorry it had to end on such a sour note." His hand reached out and tangled with several thick strands of her silky hair. "I've been wanting to do this all evening," he murmured. "I would never have believed it could be as incredibly soft as it looks, Cinderella."

Tiffany's heart leaped into her throat and lodged there. Van stood close—too close—and his eyes were too dark and intense. His head moved closer and an electric shock darted through her. Now was the time to stop this. She had to make herself turn around and unlock her door. . . .

She still hadn't moved when his fingers left her hair and encircled the back of her neck with a feather light touch. "Tiffany," he murmured as his lips grazed hers. His kiss was gentle, as if he knew he were kissing innocence, and it ended before Tiffany had a chance to react. For a moment she wondered if her legs could support her as he stepped away.

"Go sailing with me tomorrow?" he asked softly.

"Tomorrow?" She swallowed convulsively. "No . . . it's Sunday. I'm going to church. I promised Sarah Jensen I'd teach her class for her." She knew she was chattering away aimlessly. "Thanks anyway. I'll see you at work." Her hand was rummaging through her purse frantically for her key chain.

"Looking for these?" asked Van with a barely supressed chuckle in his voice. He held up her keys and she flushed as she remembered he had taken them out of her hands when they were climbing the steps a few minutes earlier.

"Yes," she said, an edge in her voice, as she attempted to take them from his hand.

His laugh was distinct now as he reached behind her, inserted the keys, and swung open her door. "See you soon, Tiff," he murmured. She slid inside the door and closed it firmly behind her, leaning against it weakly. Her heart was racing as hard as if she'd just been running from danger—danger she feared was still inside her. Her lips curved into a rueful smile. Tonight she had almost let her growing attraction to Van get the better of her.

Van walked down the steps slowly, berating himself mentally. Why was he walking out on Tiffany? Her response to him was evident; she'd been as ready to go up in flames as he was. What was there about her that made him feel so protective, made him want to put her needs above his own, made him feel murderous at the very thought of anyone's taking advantage of her loveliness?

He swung open his car door and slid in, still lost in thought. Nothing in his past experience—no other woman—had ever been more than a passionate encounter and he had always tired of them quickly.

Slowly he started his car and backed out of the parking slot. He was going to have to get a handle on this thing about Tiffany. Too much of his time was being spent thinking about her. Tomorrow, he decided, he'd take action.

CHAPTER 6

LOUISE WAS SAVING a seat for Tiffany when she arrived at the early morning church service the next day. "You look a little different," the older woman commented as the picked up her Bible and made room for Tiffany.

"I'm glad. I literally had to scrub my face raw to get all that paint off."

"It *was* glamorous . . . but I like you better this way. I want to apologize for what I was thinking last night."

"Forget it," said Tiffany.

"No, I mean it. Any kind of friend at all would have known you weren't involved in a quickie romance like that. Do you forgive me?" Louise glanced over her shoulder to scan the entrance.

"Forgiven and forgotten. Are you expecting anyone else to join us this morning?"

Louise's creamy pale complexion stained a deep

red. "Just people watching," she mumbled. "Are you still planning to teach Sarah's class this morning?"

Tiffany nodded. "Five-year-olds. I must have been crazy to agree."

"What's the lesson about?"

"Being a member of God's family. Do you think they understand that at all?"

"I don't know. But it's wonderful to start teaching them so young. Do you need my help?"

"I don't think so." Tiffany patted Louise's hand. "I wouldn't take you from your class. I know how much you're enjoying that study of Romans."

The song leader stepped forward and both women reached for a hymnal, standing on signal. Their voices combined in praise for God's goodness. Soon their own problems and concerns melted into insignificance.

By the time the message was over and they were singing the closing hymn, Tiffany felt ready to tackle anything. Even a class of wriggling five-year-olds.

Louise glanced around the auditorium with a frown. Tiffany suppressed a knowing grin. Something told her that Lou must have someone interesting she was hoping to see. A male friend?

The young adult group that had been caring for the children during the church service seemed happy to see her when she entered the room at the end of a long hall. "Children, this is Miss Martin, your teacher for today," announced a young girl with long, brown hair.

"Over to you," she whispered as she brushed past Tiffany with a grin.

"Where's my helper?" asked Tiffany.

"Oh, didn't anyone tell you? She can't make it, but

you only have a few children today. Chickenpox is going around." The girl hurried out before Tiffany could question her further.

She bit her lower lip uncertainly for a moment and then straightened her shoulders and faced the children with a bright smile. Just as the girl had said, there were only a handful of children, no more than a third of the usual number.

"Would you come up here and sit by me in these chairs in the circle so you can tell me your names?" she invited.

Thankful that the children were eager to please, she wrote out the names on colorful pieces of construction paper and clipped them to their clothing. Halfway through the session, the door opened. Tiffany glanced up and her eyes blinked in surprise. Was she seeing things? It was Van!

"Louise tells me you wouldn't mind having a little help in here today," he said.

"You? Help with Sunday school?" The words slipped out before Tiffany could catch herself. What was he doing here? How had he known what church she attended? Seeing the smile die from Van's face, she added quickly, "I mean, wouldn't you prefer to attend one of the adult classes? This might be a little elementary for you . . ."

"Probably right on my level. I'm afraid I never did attend church much as a child so I'm sure I can learn something."

"Hi," said a chubby little girl with blond ringlets. "If you tell Miss Martin your name, she'll make you a sign like mine."

Van grinned and sank down on one of the low stools. "Thank you," he said solemnly.

How was she going to live through this? She had prepared for the class, but his presence was sending every coherent thought out of her mind. There was only one thing to do, she decided. Ignore Van and make sure the kids learned all they could about being a part of God's family.

The five-year-olds were a great help. They sang the songs enthusiastically and shared information about their own families. As she prepared to go on to another activity, the blondie who had first noticed Van reminded her, "Miss Martin, you didn't ask him about his family."

"I'm sorry," said Tiffany. "Mr. Windsor, how many people are in your family?" All of the children turned round expectant eyes toward him.

"Just myself and my grandmother."

"Are you Miss Martin's daddy?" asked one of the children.

Van threw back his head and laughed, giving Tiffany a warm glance that brought a flush to her face. "Not quite."

"He means husband," corrected one of the children.

Tiffany knew she had to grab control of this situation before it got out of hand. "Children, Mr. Windsor is not my husband nor my daddy. Now let's all look up here and see our verse for the day. It's found in the Bible in a special book called Galatians. Can you say 'Galatians'?"

After giving all of them a try, she continued without risking a glance at Van. "We all love our families very much but we can be a part of God's family. In Galatians 3:26, it says, "For you are all the children of God by faith in Christ Jesus.""

Patiently, she explained the verse, portraying God as a loving Father, much like their own earthly fathers. Van sat quietly, watching her so intently she could hardly breathe. By the time the closing bell sounded, she felt as limp as a wet tissue.

Van stood beside her as the parents arrived one by one to collect the children. "They're a bunch of charmers," he said as the door closed behind the last one.

"Yes, but you can never relax a minute," sighed Tiffany. Remembering her earlier question, she asked, "What made you come here this morning?"

"I wanted to ask if you'd go sailing with me this afternoon."

"I usually help out with the teen class at night . . ."

"We can be back. It'll do you good to get a little fresh air. Run on home and change into something comfortable, and I'll pick you up in a half-hour."

The thought of a sunshiny day on board a boat was tempting. Spending time with Van wasn't so bad, either. "Thanks, I'd love it. Shall I fix us a picnic lunch?"

"I've already arranged for that if you can wait the hour or so it takes to drive to Galveston."

He had been sure of himself, hadn't he? fumed Tiffany. "I can wait," was all she said.

Louise was standing beside her car, beaming first at Tiffany and then at Van, as they approached. "How was the class?"

"A *long* hour." Louise must have known Van was coming. Had he called her after he got back to his condo last night?

"Terrific," said Van. "Tiff's a great teacher but I got insulted."

"How?" Louise seemed to be enjoying herself more than the occasion called for.

"One of the kids wanted to know if I was Tiffany's daddy."

"Oh, children that age call all men daddies," explained Louise with a laugh.

"I'll have to run if I'm going to be ready," broke in Tiffany. "Maybe Louise would like to go sailing with us, Van."

"With a redhead's complexion? I'd be fried!" Louise started toward her car. "Have a good time, you two."

For someone who had warned her against Van several times, Louise certainly seemed to have done a complete about-face, decided Tiffany as she drove toward home. When she reached her apartment she changed into a pair of white duck slacks and a new blue striped knit shirt. After tying the sleeves of a white cardigan around her shoulders, she located a pair of sunglasses and perched them on her head, more excited than was good for her, she knew. Refusing to dwell on any serious thoughts, she sat on the steps leading off the balcony in front of her apartment, humming a catchy tune as she waited.

Van arrived minutes later, dressed in worn jeans, plaid sport shirt, and a pair of leather topsiders. He bounded up the stairs and met Tiffany halfway. "Hi, gorgeous," he said. "Going my way?" Grasping both her hands, he pulled her toward him and pressed a brief, hard kiss on her lips. "Come on, I'm starving," he said a moment later, breaking the intimate moment swiftly enough that she was left breathless.

She continued to hold his hand as they went toward the car, a sleek silver sports model. "Wait a minute," said Tiffany. "How many cars do you own? This is getting ridiculous."

"Just three—the Rolls for those times when I don't want to drive, the sedan when I have several passengers, this one for when I'm with my favorite woman."

Tiffany pretended to look around. "Sorry, but I don't see her. She must have run away."

He sighed in exasperation. "Quit being difficult, Brown Eyes. We've got a long drive ahead of us."

They sped along the streets, following the intricate freeway system out of the city to sweep along the flat, swampy land leading toward the Gulf of Mexico. Tiffany flipped on the radio and found an easy listening music station. Van occasionally joined her in humming her favorite tunes.

As they crossed over a drawbridge that soared above the blue waters of the bay, Van asked, "Ever do any sailing?"

"A little. With Barry." She didn't add that her stepbrother had owned a sailboat so small it might not count in Van's eyes.

"Great. It's a perfect day for sailing. Just the right amount of breeze."

Van parked in front of a colorful marina. Boats of all sizes bobbed gently in the water—sailboats with tall graceful masts alongside bulky motor yachts and sleek racing motorboats. Tiffany slipped out of the car on her side, shielding her eyes against the sun as she waited. "Over there," directed Van.

Tiffany followed his pointing finger and saw a long white yacht. "Sailboat?" she shrilled. "That's a yacht."

"With sails," he amended. "Any objections?"

She trailed along behind him, fighting back a strange

sense of disappointment. Why wasn't she more excited about this opportunity to spend a day aboard a luxurious vessel? Surely it wasn't because she had wanted to spend the day *alone* with Van!

"It's beautiful," she managed as they strolled up the ramp. A muscular man who could have been Buck's twin greeted them.

"Carl, this is Miss Martin," said Van. "Show her around while I see about getting us underway."

Tiffany followed the man around the yacht, learning the locations of the safety equipment, the lounge, and the restrooms. *He's got this little routine down to a science,* she decided glumly. How many women had preceded her on this same tour?

Carl left her and Tiffany freshened up in the restroom before returning to the deck, leaning against the rail as the sails billowed out, carrying them far from the shore line. Her thoughts were miles away when she felt Van's arms slide around her, "Ready to eat?" his voice murmured in her ear, sending shock waves cascading through her.

Tiffany stepped aside, breaking his hold. "Starving," she said brightly. "I was beginning to think you might have forgotten."

Van gestured toward a canopied table at one end of the craft. "Everything's waiting."

It was a feast—broiled steaks, fresh garden lettuce with shredded carrots and a creamy dressing, small tender ears of corn dripping with butter. Everything was cooked to delicate perfection. Tiffany didn't know when she'd ever enjoyed a meal more. When she finished she sat back with a huge sigh. "How did you know I needed that today?"

"I know a lot about you," said Van, his gaze saying more than his words.

"I told you I'm an open book—no hidden secrets. How about you, Van? Don't you sometimes forget what's image and what's the real you?"

Her words were intended only as teasing but he took them seriously. "Yes, I do, Tiff. I think maybe that image has outlived its usefulness. In the future, I'm not going to give it any thought. Will that make you like me any better?"

"I don't dislike you," protested Tiffany.

"You just disapprove?"

She shrugged uncomfortably and was grateful when Carl appeared with a tray of fresh fruit. Choosing a ripe, red strawberry, Tiffany popped it in her mouth to preclude further conversation. Her feelings about the magnificence of this yacht must have shown too clearly. Who was she to think she had a right to criticize anyone else?

Van seemed content to leave it at that and when they finished off a good portion of the fruit on the tray, they wandered over to the railing. "Sure you need to get back for that class tonight?" he asked, his lips against her hair, his hand lightly touching her waist.

"Certain, Van. It's been a wonderful afternoon. Have you ever taken any long cruises in your yacht?"

"No more than a week. That's the longest I've had to spare."

She turned slightly and his hand tightened on her waist, drawing her closer against him. "Why? Why do you work such long hours when you already have everything you could possibly want, Van?" she asked, ignoring his nearness as best she could. If she struggled she knew it would only amuse him. Better to let him think he had no effect on her. She was still humiliated over the way she'd melted when he'd touched her the evening before.

His lips brushed her neck in soft, silky exploration. "Not everything," he whispered. "I've been wanting to hold you in my arms since the day I met you. Why are you fighting me, Brown Eyes?"

She was proud to be able to move away with a teasing laugh. "Fighting you, Van? I thought I was being quite friendly. Maybe it's just that we have different ideas of what friendship means."

Hooded dark eyes stared her down. "Friendship," he mocked. "Who's been talking about friendship, Tiff?"

She felt a sharp stab of disappointment, followed by anger. "Maybe I need my hearing checked. What are you offering, Van? A whirlwind romance? Champagne, parties, gifts in exchange for some lovemaking? Maybe you haven't noticed that those things don't mean much to me."

"What *is* important to you, Tiff? What can I do to break down that wall you keep throwing up?"

Tiffany watched him silently. How could she explain in a few words the gulf between them? As she'd taught the children that morning, she was a member of God's family and Van was not. But anything she might say would sound as if she felt herself superior. That wasn't the issue at all.

He laughed cynically and turned to stare out at the sea. "So that's it. You're just too kind to say I don't turn you on. I guess I was fooled last night. Well, I hope this won't keep us from working together to solve the mystery of the missing information, anyway."

She had to fight with every ounce of strength in her not to reach out with a comforting gesture. "I'm as anxious as you are to find out who's guilty," she said quietly. "It would mean a lot to me if we could be friends. Everyone else at the company respects you, and I understand why. You're a terrific person, Van, not at all the way I thought when we first met."

"Good old Tiff," he murmured. "Can't stand to have to hurt anyone." He turned to face her. "Spare the pity. I find your usual bluntness more refreshing."

His belief that she found him somehow unappealing might have been funny if her pain would have allowed her to laugh. If only she'd never met him . . . if only she'd never taken over Barry's job . . . She stopped herself short. Such thoughts were wrong—almost as if she wasn't thankful for God's plan for her life. "Then don't blame me the next time I forget you're my boss and say exactly what I'm thinking," she said with a shaky laugh.

"It's a promise," he agreed, his lips curving into that gentle smile that melted her. "*Pax*, Tiff?" he held out his hand.

"*Pax*," she agreed, clasping his fingers tightly.

Tiffany invited several friends over for coffee and cake after the church service that evening. Louise lingered after the others left, insisting she wanted to help with the clean-up operations. They worked together as an efficient team and within minutes the last cup and saucer was clean and put away. "I don't know about you but this weekend has been anything but restful," said Tiffany, stifling a yawn.

"But you did have fun?" Louise's blue eyes studied Tiffany intently.

"It was a chance to see how the other half lives."

"And you do enjoy being with Van?"

Tiffany sighed in exasperation. "Louise, nothing's going to happen between Van and me. Of course, I find him attractive and exciting. Who wouldn't? But you're the very one who warned me not to take him seriously."

"Oh, I've changed my mind. I can tell he's interested in you . . ."

"Not in *me*—in only one thing," Tiffany reminded dryly.

"Maybe you're being too cynical. Why don't you at least give him a chance?"

Tiffany led the way into her small living area and flopped down on the sofa. "Tell me what changed your mind this drastically."

Louise perched on the edge of the overstuffed chair. "He came to church this morning," she pointed out.

"He likes a challenge. I told him I couldn't go sailing with him because I was going to church. He just couldn't bear not being the winner." Tiffany leaned forward. "Let's just drop this subject for a while. How about any suspects at work? Did you and Joss think of anyone?"

Louise reached for her purse from a nearby table and dug into it eagerly, pulling out a piece of paper. She handed it over to Tiffany with a smug expression on her face. "We're going about this in a systematic fashion. In the center of the page we've written Bob Hartman's name because Joss and I are both convinced he's the main culprit. Then around the page is the name of every employee in the company. The dotted lines linking them to Bob's name indicate their connection with him in some way. Do you see the name with the most lines?''

''Mabel Roan?'' Tiffany remembered the small, gray-haired woman who worked in the accounting department with Dave Allredge. ''What's her connection?''

''Her husband is a tailor. He makes some of Bob Nelson's clothes.''

''What would be her access to the files?''

Louise pulled out another sheet of paper. ''This is the other side. In the center is the file. As you can see, Mabel's name doesn't have a single line connecting her with that.''

''So she's eliminated.''

''Almost,'' admitted Louise. ''Our prime suspects at this time are Dave, Buck, and Pam.''

''Pam?'' Tiffany couldn't help laughing. ''Pam can't even remember the topics of my research papers, much less be secretive enough to run a highly organized spy operation.''

Louise shrugged. ''I agree, but Joss insisted on putting her name there. Frankly, both Joss and I think the most likely ones are Dave or Buck.''

''Have you told Van?''

''Joss was meeting with him this evening. I've had an idea and wonder what you think. How about putting out some false information and seeing who takes the bait?''

''Brilliant,'' laughed Tiffany. ''Maybe you missed your calling in life.''

'' 'Baker's Detective Agency.' That does have a

99

nice ring to it," said Louise with a twinkle in her eye. "Would you work for me?"

"I wouldn't be any good at all. It's making me sick inside to even think Dave or Buck might be involved in this. Couldn't it possibly be an outside source? The cleaning crew that comes each evening? The security force for the building? Have you investigated all those?"

"Thoroughly. The way things are handled I believe we can eliminate anyone who isn't an employee of Windsor Enterprises." Louise put the papers back into her purse. "Now that you know what we're working on, I'd like your help. If you see or hear anything that might be relevant, let me know so I can put it on these charts."

"At your service, ma'am," said Tiffany before giving into an overwhelming urge to yawn.

"Was that a hint?" said Louise, laughing as she stood to her feet.

"I'm sorry to be so dull." Tiffany followed her to the door. "See you at work tomorrow, Louise."

"Sweet dreams about yachts and a handsome sailor called Van."

"That's the last thing I need to dream about," answered Tiffany, giving her friend a playful shove to hurry her on her way.

CHAPTER 7

TRYING TO RECALL if this was the day she had arranged to tour the solar energy research center, Tiffany walked into the outer office the next morning. She spun to a stop, doing her best to stifle a grin at the sight of the striped tent dress Pam was wearing.

"Go ahead, say it," moaned Pam. "Everyone coming through those doors has made some crack about my new dress."

"It *is* colorful," said Tiffany most diplomatically.

"I let the salesclerk talk me into it," explained Pam. "You know that book I read about how to marry a rich husband said to wear something that attracts attention. I guess it meant the right kind of attention, huh?"

Tiffany laughed as she unlocked her desk drawer and removed a disk. "Have a good weekend?"

"Terrible. I waited all weekend for one call from someone special. It never came. How about you?"

The switchboard lights came on and Pam answered.

Her eyes were narrow slits when she turned to face Tiffany. "Now's that's the last straw. Bob Hartman is on line one and he wants to speak to *you*."

"Tell him I'm busy and he can leave a message."

After doing as Tiffany had directed, Pam swiveled her chair around. "What's going on? Are you trying to corner the market on rich, available men?"

Tiffany didn't glance up, thumbing through some papers to locate where she'd left off work on Friday. "Do you know Bob?"

"I'm the one who introduced you to him at that party Louise took us to a couple of months ago, remember? Aren't you even curious about what he wants?"

"Not especially. He didn't impress me much. Too conceited."

"He's that, all right." Pam sauntered over with a slip of paper in her hand. "Here's the number he left."

Tiffany tried to keep her voice casual. "Do you know him well?"

"I've been to a couple of parties at his house. Pretty wild affairs, if you know what I mean."

"How long ago?"

"Not recently. I wish I'd get another invitation. He lives in a fantastic garden home. There's even an indoor swimming pool," Pam sighed enviously. "Are you going to call him?"

Tiffany shook her head. "No, but if he calls again, I'll talk to him so you won't be in the middle." Should she report Pam's remarks about Bob to Louise? Surely if the young girl had anything to hide, she wouldn't be talking so freely about him.

It was after ten before her phone buzzed and Pam

informed her Bob was on line two. Tiffany picked up the receiver. "Research Department. Tiffany Martin."

"So it's really you," said the smooth, urbane voice. "When I first heard that a gorgeous gal like you was actually head of Van's research department, I refused to believe it."

"Mr. Hartman, I'm quite busy now. What was it you wanted?"

He laughed. "I called to apologize."

"I can't imagine why."

"For the other evening. I didn't mean my remarks about your necklace to be offensive. Am I forgiven?"

"Why not? Was there anything else you needed?"

"Miss Martin . . . please . . . I'm really sincere about being sorry. Could we have lunch together today so I can prove it?"

"I'm afraid not. I already have an engagement. Let's just consider the matter forgotten."

"That's very generous of you." His pause was brief. "May I call again soon and see if you're free?"

She was ready to refuse when she realized that Van might want her to keep the lines open between Bob and herself during the investigation. "If you'd like, but I can't promise anything."

Pam was leaning on her desk as she replaced the receiver. "What did he want?"

"Lunch." At Pam's furiously hurt look she added, "Pam, I don't have a smidgen of interest in Bob."

"But it's not fair. First, Van and now, Bob. And you don't even try." Tears welled up in the blue eyes, and one slid down her cheek and plopped onto the front of her striped dress.

Tiffany was on her feet in a second, hugging Pam

against her. "Please don't feel bad. Men like that aren't worth crying over. They don't even care about the important things . . . all the luncheon dates in the world don't guarantee happiness."

"I'd like to try out that theory," Pam managed between sobs that were gradually diminishing. She stepped back and scrubbed her face with the back of her fist. "I guess my mascara's running. Now I must really look like a circus clown."

"What you need is a good lunch with some friends. I'll handle the switchboard while you clean up. When you come back, I expect you to have picked the most exciting dining spot in Houston. Louise and I will take you."

Pam gulped and then giggled. "I'd like that a lot, Tiff."

Louise was less sympathetic when Tiffany explained the situation. "Of course I'll be glad to go to lunch with you two but I think you're being too soft on the girl. She's refused dates with a couple of nice young men I've introduced her to."

"I didn't say I approved of her thinking, Lou."

The older woman's voice softened. "Okay, so I am being a little tough. Anyway, I want to pursue this interest in Bob Hartman. It may be our first solid lead in the case."

Just before lunch a florist arrived, carrying one perfect white rose in a crystal vase. "Over there," said Pam in a tight voice, pointing across the room to the alcove where Tiffany was working.

Tiffany thanked the delivery man and sat staring at the delicate flower for several moments before reaching for the card. "Thanks for making my day the best. Van," she read, slipping it back in its envelope as

Pam started toward her. Ignoring her racing pulses, she turned to face her.

"Another admirer?" said the receptionist.

"Van."

Pam's voice was shrill. "Oh, just old Van, huh? You're really getting good at this, Tiffany. Maybe you can write a book about it soon."

"Sarcasm is not becoming, Pam. Who's your switchboard relief? I made our reservations for twelve-fifteen. We better leave."

Pam was in a much better mood by the time they returned. "I guess my problem was I spent the weekend alone. Maybe I'll take you up on coming to your singles class next weekend."

"We'd love to have you," answered Tiffany as she gathered up her notebook and purse for her trip to the solar research institute that afternoon. She was ready to leave when the phone on her desk buzzed. It was Van. "If you're free, I'd like to see you in my office for a few minutes, Tiff."

"Yes. Right away," she said, determined not to let Pam know where she was going.

Van was sitting on the leather Chippendale loveseat on one side of his office, his dark head bent over an open briefcase containing a number of papers. He glanced up with a smile, causing Tiffany's heart to do a series of rapid flipflops.

As he started to rise, Tiffany motioned to him. "Don't bother." She sat down across a polished mahogany table from him. "What did you need?"

He leaned back, his long, powerful legs stretched out, his dark eyes flickering over her and glinting with approval. "I think I needed to see you. I've been doing a lot of thinking about what you said."

Just what was he referring to? She remembered saying many things in the last few days . . . some of which she wasn't so proud of. "And what conclusions did you draw?" she probed nervously.

He chuckled. "That you interest me very much, Miss Martin. Now, for business. I hear you reeled in our fish today."

"Bob?"

He nodded grimly. "Louise tells me he called and asked you to lunch."

"I refused."

"Good. I've decided to pull you off this case. Joss and I . . ."

"Hold on," interrupted Tiffany. "I'm very much involved in this. Why have you changed your mind? It's obvious your plan is already beginning to work. I want to help; I can't rest easy until we know the truth."

"Sorry. You heard my orders."

"Orders?" Tiffany was seething inside over his rude dismissal. Or was there more to this than he was saying? Had he learned something that made him suspect once again she might be the guilty party?

"Orders," he repeated firmly.

"What exactly are my orders?" she said between clenched teeth.

"You're to forget all I've told you. You're to cut Hartman off the next time he calls."

"And what if I refuse? What if I continue to investigate this on my own time?"

His eyes narrowed. "You have a personal reason for wanting to see Hartman again?"

"Van!" Tiffany stood, glaring down at him. "I don't think you're leveling with me. Something's

106

come up that you don't trust me to know, so you're shutting me out." Her voice began to quaver with frustration. "I'm not making any promises about whom I see away from work."

Van stood, towering over her, returning glare for glare. "And I'm not making any promises what I'll do to Hartman if I ever catch him around you!"

"Then that's *his* problem!" Tiffany hurried over to the door and shut it before she said any more. She was back at her desk before she remembered she hadn't thanked him for the rose. Too late now, she realized and, with tears blurring her vision, she left the office.

That evening she tried to sort out what had happened to make everything go wrong. What was the real reason behind Van's request for her not to see Bob again? For a moment she allowed herself to indulge in the fantasy that it might be jealousy. Shaking her head so vigorously it sent the blond hair swirling over her shoulders, she laughed lightly. That would certainly be living in a fool's paradise. No, Van was suspicious of her once more, and he didn't intend to let her know how the investigation was going. That thought hurt. How could she defend herself if she didn't even know what she'd done wrong?

The sight of the rose on her desk the next morning brought on a new bout of guilt. She hurried down to the newsstand in the lobby of the building and purchased a small note card with a sailboat on the front. After writing a brief thank-you message she carried it down the hall to Louise's desk. "Will you please give this to Van?"

"Give it to him yourself," said Louise. She pointed

toward the door. "I just took him in a cup of coffee, so I know he's not too busy."

"No . . . I'd rather . . ." Feeling foolish, Tiffany turned and started toward his door.

Van jumped to his feet and strode across the room when Tiffany walked in, grabbing both of her hands and pulling her toward him. "I was just thinking of you, Tiff. You're looking lovely this morning." His lips were almost against her cheek.

A warm current pulsated through Tiffany in time with the beating of her heart. "I'm afraid I got so rattled yesterday I forgot to thank you for the rose. It's exquisite, Van."

His gaze traced the lines of her face in an intimate caress. "Like its owner. I hope you're not still upset with me."

She forced herself to step back. "I'll agree to keep Bob Hartman from taking up any of the time when I'm on your payroll," she said crisply.

His eyes hinted at amusement. "That puts me in my place fairly neatly. How's the report on solar energy coming?"

"I have the rough draft finished and am working on my revisions now."

"Good. I'll be ready to start work on that project when I return from my trip to the Netherlands. I'm leaving tomorrow."

Going away? Tiffany felt a keen disappointment but she maintained a cool façade. "Sounds like an interesting place to visit."

"And Tiff," he said, pulling her against him and kissing her before she had a chance to react, "when I get back, we'll have dinner together. I think I can convince you we're not as far apart in our thinking as you seem determined to think."

"Take care," she murmured, doubting that anything Van said could close the chasm that seemed to be widening between them.

Throughout the day the sky grew increasingly dark, churning with menacing clouds. By five, thunder began rumbling as Tiffany started across the vast parking lot to the slot where her car was parked. Halfway there, rain began pelting down, huge drops blown by strong, gusty winds. Holding her briefcase as a protective shield in front of her, she began running.

Footsteps pounded behind her. "This way," shouted Van. With one arm around her he steered her toward his own car and propelled her inside.

"Why does it always have to start raining just as it's time to go home?" asked Tiffany, frantically wiping droplets of moisture from her arms.

"Don't ask me. Where are you parked?"

"Over there . . ." She stopped as an electronic beeping signaled a call on his radiophone.

Van spoke rapidly and then replaced the receiver. "That's a relief. The dinner party I thought I had to attend has been called off." A smile spread across his chiseled features. "I've got a great idea. Why don't you come to my place for dinner tonight?"

"Oh, I couldn't."

"Why not? Were you going out?"

"No, but I'm . . . too wet." she said, grabbing for the first excuse that came to mind. She wasn't exactly certain what a dinner invitation at Van's place included, but it was probably better not to take any chances of a misunderstanding.

There was a glint of amusement in Van's eyes. "Scared of me?"

"Should I be?" she countered lightly.

He smiled lazily. "Tiff, please come to dinner. Mrs. Duncan loves cooking for guests. We'll listen to records, get to know each other better. Rainy evenings are meant to be shared."

"As friends?"

"Friends," he agreed, starting the powerful engine of the sports car.

Who am I trying to fool? Tiffany thought wryly as they exited from the parking lot. Friendship was not on Van's mind. He had made no bones about their chances of being friends on his yacht. But she need never be afraid of him; he'd never have to force his attentions on any woman—not with such effective weapons at his disposal.

Still wondering what had possessed her to agree to his invitation, she studied his profile covertly, noting the even perfection of his features, the strong jawline that spoke of a relentless determination. Outside, the fierceness of the storm intensified their closeness in the small car and she steeled herself against a quiver of longing to move nearer to him.

Van felt her gaze and turned to her. "Hungry?"

"Starving."

"What would you have eaten tonight? More junk food?"

"Everyone doesn't have a housekeeper ready to cater to his slightest whim."

An enchantingly crooked smile softened his mouth. "Are you accusing me of laziness, Miss Martin?"

Her eyes widened in mock innocence. "Don't try putting words in my mouth, Mr. Windsor."

When they reached Van's penthouse apartment, it was silent, an air of icy desolation in the darkened rooms. "Mrs. Duncan," called Van.

Tiffany followed him down the marble-floored hallway to one small pinpoint of light from a lamp. Propped beside it was a note. Van read it quickly and then handed it to Tiffany. "It looks like we'll have to go out. Mrs. Duncan's sister is ill and she's gone to the hospital to visit her."

Without thinking, Tiffany blurted out, "I know how to cook. Besides, it wouldn't hurt you to learn your way around a kitchen." Too late she caught the gleam in Van's eyes. Did he think she wanted to spend this evening alone with him?

"You're on. What are you going to teach me?"

She'd just have to bluff her way through this, she decided. "Let's see what's available in the way of groceries."

"Want to change into something more comfortable?" His voice was laden with suggestion.

She glanced down at the soft fabric of her dress, which had dried completely, pretending to misunderstand. "As you can see, this dress takes a lot of punishment."

The flicker of amusement in his eyes showed she hadn't fooled him. "Then give me a few minutes to change." Pointing toward the solarium, he added, "Make yourself at home in there until I get back."

Tiffany settled down on the sofa, leaning back and watching huge drops of rain splattering on the glass dome. A feeling of contentment stole over her and her mind drifted into a dreamy state, wondering what it

111

would be like to be spending an evening like this with a man she loved. Her long lashes fluttered downward as she drifted into sleep.

Something brushed against her cheek, awakening her, but she fought against it, burrowing deeper into the soft, cushions of the sofa. *Sofa?* She sat up, blinking, aware that sofas didn't have the clean, masculine lime-scented aroma that she had been reveling in. Van's face was so near it blurred her vision, his arm was encircling her and she must have been resting her head on his shoulder. With a heart beating so loudly she was certain he had to be aware of it, she moved away, brushing back her hair with shaky fingers.

"You have a beautiful face," murmured Van.

"I can't believe I fell asleep."

"I'm glad you did; you were relaxed around me for a change, Tiff. Do you know no one else has ever placed me in the role of ogre before?"

Her mouth curved into a gentle smile. "Does it fit?"

"I'd be less than truthful if I said I didn't want to make love to you," he said, his voice becoming more husky with each word. "Your hair drives me wild . . . it's so soft and tempting . . ."

"Van . . . please . . ." How could a man's words have the power to make her feel this way?

He sighed, leaning back. "I see you're fully awake now. Don't worry, I haven't forgotten that my invitation was for dinner."

"And I offered to cook it with your help," she said, jumping to her feet. Tugging on his hand, she added, "Come on. You're not going to escape that lesson I promised you."

112

"There are lots more interesting things to learn," he grumbled good-naturedly as he followed her down the hall.

Tiffany searched through a well-stocked pantry and refrigerator. "You've got a mini-grocery store here. Do you entertain much?"

"No, but when I do, Mrs. Duncan never has much notice so she tries to keep everything on hand."

"Will she mind my working in here? Some women are quite jealous over their kitchens."

"She'd be delighted to see that you are trying to domesticate me."

"Yes, I do have a talent for pursuing lost causes," returned Tiffany with a grin. After pulling open several drawers, she located two aprons and pitched one to Van. "Put this on and I'll give you some potatoes to peel."

With an expressive roll of his eyes, Van complied. "Mind showing me how?"

He was an apt student. As she removed a package of pork chops from the freezer, he leaned industriously over the sink, the powerful muscles of his arms rippling with each deft movement. Tiffany hid a grin that threatened to erupt over the thought of what his friends would think if they could see him now.

When she had finished breading the chops and had placed them on a sizzling hot griddle, she glanced over at Van, her eyes rounding at the rapidly growing pile of potatoes. "Two," she managed before breaking into peals of cascading laughter.

"Two? Is that all?"

"That's more than enough unless you're preparing to feed an army." She located a bowl and scooped up the surplus, covering them with water before placing them in the refrigerator. "Tell Mrs. Duncan that you attacked that sack of potatoes like it was a company you were intent on acquiring."

By the time the chops were a golden brown and the potatoes had been mashed and laced with melting dabs of butter, Tiffany felt her stomach rumbling with hunger. Van had become caught up in the adventure, offering to toss crisp, fresh greens with an Italian dressing for their salad. When he finished he set two plates on a round table in front of a bay window in the kitchen. "How am I doing?" he asked as he pulled out a chair for her with a flourish.

"Not bad for someone who's never had to lift a finger in a kitchen before. I suspect you've been spoiled."

"Call it deprived. This is fun. Think you could set up a regular schedule of these lessons?"

"I'm not sure the potato farmers can meet the demand." She ducked as Van reached out to ruffle her hair in protest.

There was silence as they concentrated on the food until Van began complimenting her efforts. "This is great, Tiff. You're a woman of many talents."

"Thanks. Maybe the secret is to be so hungry that everything tastes delicious."

A bell chimed from the rear of the kitchen. "What's that?" asked Tiffany.

"Delivery entrance." Van spoke into an intercom. "Who's there?"

"Dave Allredge. I brought the contract on the Murray deal."

Tiffany opened her mouth to warn Van that he was still wearing his apron, but too late. He strode over and swung open a door.

114

"I didn't expect you to be here," said Dave, his eyes gradually widening as they encountered first the apron and then the cozy domestic scene. "Tiff . . ." he began, his face suffused with a dull brick red color. "I hope I'm not interrupting anything, Van."

Tiffany gave up her battle to remain quiet and dissolved into laughter. "What's so funny?" demanded Van.

"Your apron. Dave's face . . ." Her laughter increased to a point where she couldn't continue.

Dave joined in, both he and Tiffany laughing even harder as Van whipped off the offending garment and pitched it onto the counter. "What's the matter with you two? Haven't you ever seen a man in an apron before?"

"Not you!" chortled Dave when he managed to catch his breath. "How did you get it on him, Tiff?"

"A little lasso trick I learned one summer when I worked on a ranch," she drawled. It was fun to see Van sputtering for words once. "How about joining us, Dave? Van's mashed potatoes are fantastic."

"Okay, you two," said Van, the sternness of his tone completely out of keeping with the twinkle in his eyes. "What kind of blackmail are you scheming? If either of you brings out a camera, I'm going to swear I was set up."

Mrs. Duncan arrived in the middle of the hilarity. "Why, Mr. Windsor," she exclaimed. "I had no idea you were having guests or I'd never have left you. Did you call a catering firm?" Dave and Tiffany erupted into another, louder round of laughter.

"Windsor's Catering Services. I can just see it now," said Dave, bringing on another outburst of laughter.

"Don't mind these two, Mrs. Duncan," said Van. "I think they got into the cooking sherry by mistake." He picked up the bowl of potatoes and held them out for the housekeeper's inspection. "You are now looking at the results of my first cooking effort. Not bad if I do say so."

"Don't forget to tell her about the ones in the refrigerator." Tiffany fought to keep from laughing. At the look of bewilderment on the elderly woman's face she rose and went over to her. "I'm afraid all this mess in your kitchen is my fault. I challenged Van to a cooking contest, and you know how he never passes up a dare."

Mrs. Duncan's face broke into a smile. "And it's about time he learned a little. Don't let me interrupt, dear."

"How's your sister?" asked Van.

"Doing well. The doctor says she's improving."

Dave accepted Tiffany's invitation to join them for coffee, but he excused himself as soon as he drained the last drop. "I don't want to interrupt anything . . ." The tone of his voice made his meaning crystal-clear.

Tiffany's mood sobered as she realized the gossip that would be floating around the office by the next morning. After Dave left, she attempted to clear away the dishes but Mrs. Duncan returned, insisting that she wanted to take over.

"Run along, dearie, while I put these in the dishwasher. I always like a little exercise before I go to bed. Makes me sleep better."

Van nodded when Tiffany asked if he would drive her to the parking lot so she could get her car. On the ride over he did most of the talking, discussing his upcoming trip to the Netherlands. When they arrived at the office, he waited until she started her car and then waved as he drove off. A dull ache settled in the pit of Tiffany's stomach. She was going to miss him while he was gone. She realized she had allowed him to become important to her. How had that happened?

CHAPTER 8

BY FRIDAY MORNING Tiffany was so restless she couldn't concentrate. Impatient with herself for her preoccupation with Van, she reached for a note pad. She'd spend the morning at the university library doing more research on solar energy . . . the rough draft of her report was still sketchy in places.

After telling Pam not to expect her back until after lunch, she waved to Louise and then hurried to the parking lot. "Charlie," her ancient car, refused to cooperate. She gave up in exasperation after several futile attempts to start it, and was climbing out when a shining red convertible pulled up beside her.

"Just my luck," yelled Bob Hartman, his blond hair gleaming in the bright sunlight. "I was on my way to your office to see if I could talk you into having lunch with me at the Inn-on-the-Park today."

"It's not even ten," pointed out Tiffany, still fuming over her car's balky behavior.

"Were you just arriving?" asked Bob, ignoring the lack of welcome in her cool tones.

"No, leaving. I'm on my way to Rice University, but my car's giving a little trouble." She turned her back on him and began gathering up her supplies from the front seat of her car.

"How about a ride? I'll drop you off and come back at lunchtime."

Van's stern look as he had ordered her not to see Bob Hartman again swept through her mind. On the verge of refusing, she listened as Bob added, "A little bird told me you're researching an interest of mine . . . solar energy."

Excitement swept through Tiffany. Perhaps if she pretended friendliness she might find out who that "little bird" was. "You're never going to believe this, but my boss told me not to have anything to do with you," she said with a show of hesitancy.

Bob's white teeth gleamed as he laughed loudly. "Jealous of me, is he? I hear he's out of town so why does he need to know? Or does he have some claim on you that gives him the right to choose your friends for you?"

Tiffany smiled mentally at this attempt of Bob's to put a wedge between Van and herself—as if any woman would have any difficulty choosing between the two men. "No claims at all," she said lightly.

Bob leaned over and opened the door of the convertible. Tiffany slid in, carefully adjusting her skirt to cover the expanse of leg her actions had revealed. Bob's eyes gleamed appreciatively.

"Old Windsor's been neglecting you a bit lately, has he?"

She shrugged and he chuckled.

"You don't have to say anything. I know how he treats his women. 'Love 'em and leave 'em Windsor,' we used to call him in college."

Petty, that's what he is, she decided, disliking him more with each passing moment. If there was one thing that she despised, it was hearing someone run down people behind their backs.

"Are you going to waste a beautiful day like this talking about Van Windsor?" she asked with a bright smile.

He reached over but she deflected his hand with a light slap before it contacted her knee. The smile he gave her didn't quite reach his eyes as he drew back. "I understand Barry Nelson was your stepbrother."

"Your little bird does a lot of squawking," said Tiffany. "What's your interest in what goes on at Windsor Enterprises?"

"Oh, didn't you know? Van and I are lifelong friends."

She laughed, matching his sarcasm. "I wouldn't have guessed. What do you really have against Van?"

Bob's eyes narrowed. "Our feud started a long time ago. Why don't you ask Van?"

"I'm not that interested. What do you do for a living, Bob?"

"My dad and I have a financial services firm. We recommend investments for our clients."

"Mmm, sounds terrifically impressive," Tiffany attempted to sound the way Pam would in the same circumstances.

"It is," said Bob. "Dump Windsor and I'll show you what a good time is."

"That's a tempting offer," managed Tiffany, relieved to see the ivy-covered brick walls of one of the

120

main buildings on the Rice University campus looming ahead. "What time will you be back to pick me up?"

"Eleven forty-five?"

"Great. I've never been to the Inn-on-the-Park but I've heard it's fabulous." She climbed out of the car and waved before hurrying inside the building.

For some reason she couldn't get down to work, a niggling sense of guilt invading her mind. What was her problem? She hadn't promised Van she'd stay away from Bob Hartman. This might be the break they'd all been looking for. If she played her part right, there was a slight possibility she could pick up some valuable clues. With that reassuring thought, she banished the nagging worries and hurried over to one of the librarians for help in dialing up an information service on the university's large computer.

Bob was waiting for her when she came outside two hours later. "Ready, beautiful?" he murmured.

The Inn-on-the-Park was everything Tiffany had heard. The hotel was situated at Four Riverway on the edge of a beautifully tended park filled with lushly green trees. A silvery pond lay like a jewel in the center of the park, a perfect setting for the graceful swans and paddling ducks.

The restaurant Bob had chosen was a picture of discreet elegance. The decor was quietly understated, the beveled glass French doors, fresh flowers, fine china, and spotless crystal, creating an ambiance of exquisitely fine taste and unlimited capital. The contrast between Bob's and Van's styles was evident when they entered the restaurant. Bob patted the table captain on the back in a patronizing manner and made several demands that bordered on rudeness. Cringing inside, Tiffany tried to keep up a bright smile, determined to learn something that would make her feel she hadn't made a mistake in agreeing to this luncheon.

After a long conference in French with the waiter, Bob placed their orders. For appetizers he chose sautéed escargot, which, he explained in a superior voice, were snails in a garlic sauce. Tiffany started to remind him that she knew French—it had been her minor in college—but she decided that Bob must need to think women were all dumb little creatures.

When their food arrived, Tiffany exclaimed over it and saw that Bob was enjoying this chance to play the role of teacher. Flattery, she guessed, would be the method that would extract information from him.

"This is such a treat," she said several times. "You're really an exciting person, Bob."

"Think nothing of it, sweetheart. This is only the beginning of the good times I'm going to show you."

Quelling her shudder of distaste, Tiffany nodded.

The next course was delicious—delicately browned slices of tenderloin of lamb over layers of spinach and fresh mushrooms, covered by a buttery sauce laced with truffles. It was so tender it needed no knife. With her words carefully thought out, Tiffany began to probe. "Do you know a lot of people who work at Windsor's?"

"Why, babe? Worried that someone will tell Van you had lunch with me?" he teased.

She lowered her eyes and pretended to concentrate on her food. "He won't like it if he finds out."

"Then let's keep it all to ourselves. Our own little secret. Say, I've got a great little place down on the coast where just you and I could go this week-end . . ."

Tiffany couldn't prevent the icy stare that glazed her eyes.

"Okay," added Bob placatingly. "Maybe I'm moving a little fast for you. How about coming to a party at my house tomorrow night?"

"Pam says your parties are on the wild side."

"Pam?" His look was pure innocence and Tiffany felt a sense of relief. Pam was obviously not his source at Windsor's.

"Our receptionist. She said she went to a party at your place."

He hit his head in mock dismay. "Please don't tell her I can't remember her. I never like to have a lady mad at me."

For dessert, the waiter brought out thin slices of chocolate raspberry torte with cups of coffee.

Feeling almost desperate, Tiffany tried once more. "I don't know about that party. Will there be anyone I know there?"

Bob ran his hand down her bare arm lightly, sending another shiver of revulsion through her. "Scared of me, Tiff? That receptionist of yours must have told some tall tales."

"I'm not into anything wild," she said quietly, giving him a piercing look that underlined her words.

He nodded with a returning seriousness. "I guessed that. Would you believe it if I told you I'm looking for stability in a woman, Tiffany?"

"Not really," she answered, taking a sip of her coffee. "I think you'd find me extremely boring." Glancing at her watch, she gasped. "I'm late, Bob. Please take me back to the office."

Bob's gray eyes flared with anger. "Eat and run?"

"Were there strings attached to this invitation?" Tiffany didn't know when she'd ever disliked a man more. How could any woman find him charming company? He was the most conceited—the most selfish . . .

With only a cold glance in her direction, he signaled to the waiter. When they reached the lobby of the hotel, Tiffany moved away from him. "On second thought, I've decided to take a taxi back to work." She strode over to a red-jacketed bellman and gave him her request, with Bob standing tensely beside her.

As the bellman moved away to locate a taxi for her, Bob grasped her arm, his lip curling in fury. "What's all this about? You were willing enough to accept a ride to the library and this lunch. Now that you've gotten what you want, you're walking out on me."

Tiffany pulled her arm away. "I find your company repulsive," she said.

Why hadn't she listened to Van? He had only been trying to warn her for her own good. Bob Hartman was the type of person who flourished on ego and would hold a grudge against anyone who dared to wound his fragile vanity. He wasn't honest enough to fight out in the open, but preyed on others' weaknesses to get what he wanted from them. Tiffany realized with a chilling certainty that she had made a dangerous enemy.

With a face mottled with rage, Bob stepped away, saying in a low, menacing undertone. "You're going to pay for this. Van isn't going to like the rumors he hears about you and me."

"Van will consider the source," Tiffany returned with more confidence than she was feeling.

It was a foggy evening in Amsterdam. Van ignored the invitation in the young woman's voice as she let him off in front of his hotel. After the dinner party at her father's home where he had finalized a business deal, she had insisted on driving him here. Her long straight blond hair swished from side to side as she cast coy looks in his direction and rapidly suggested places they could go where the night life might interest him. He hoped his ruse of appearing to be having difficulty understanding her halting English might soften what amounted to a rejection.

When he reached the luxurious hotel room, he showered and stretched out on the soft bed, staring around him morosely. When had he ever felt so empty and alone before? The image of Tiffany's luminous brown eyes and the champagne-blond hair curling softly around her face pirouetted into his head. He groaned, imagining the feel of the feminine curves and tantalizing lips.

He rolled over and reached for his wallet from the dresser, extracting a card with Tiffany's phone number. Should he call her? Every day since they'd been, apart he had been fighting this same battle. What held him back? Was he afraid he'd reveal how much she was coming to mean to him?

Angry over the trend of his thoughts, he reached for the phone, asking for the international operator. When the connections were made, he waited tensely as the phone rang several times. On the verge of hanging up, he heard a soft voice. "Hello."

"Tiff. Van." For some strange reason his throat constricted.

"Van!" There was no doubt of the welcome in her voice.

"Did I wake you?" He didn't know when he'd felt better.

"No, I've already walked to the grocery store this morning."

"That sounds energetic."

"Necessity. My car had to be towed in and it's getting a new starter."

"You could call Buck, and he'd bring you one of mine for as long as you need it."

"Thanks, but no." Her heart was beginning to beat more normally now. "how are things in the Netherlands? Seen any wooden shoes lately?"

"Not around here. The weather's been gloomy, but business is terrific."

"When are you coming back?"

"I'm leaving in the morning. I'll take the direct flight to Houston. How about dinner at my place tomorrow night? Mrs. Duncan asked me to have you over soon."

"I'd love it. Maybe you can whip up a few more of those mashed potatoes for us."

"Okay . . . enough of those remarks."

Tiffany laughed. "What time?"

"My plane is due to arrive there about six. Why don't I have Buck pick you up . . ."

"That's Sunday. Our singles class will be out about eight-thirty. Is that too late?"

"It's perfect. How have you been, Brown Eyes?" His voice dropped several decibels, the warm, caressing tone setting off explosions inside Tiffany.

"Busy. You?"

"Missing you."

She felt as light-headed as if Van had kissed her. "Is that flattery?"

126

"Truth."

After a long pause, he added, "Why none of your usual flippant remarks, Tiff?"

Why, indeed? Because I'm a fool, thought Tiffany. *I've fallen in love with you. Just hearing your voice makes me weak and fluttery inside and I'm finding it hard to remember why we're not for each other.*

"This is my first international call and I'm a little nervous," she admitted.

His laugh was tender. "You're so refreshingly honest, Tiffany. No attempt to appear blasé and sophisticated. Your parents must have been terrific people to have a son and daughter like you and Barry."

Tears welled in her eyes over the unexpected praise for the parents she missed so sorely. "They were wonderful." With an attempt to pull herself together, she added in a more forceful tone, "Isn't this costing you a fortune?"

"It's worth every guilder but since it's nearly midnight here, I guess I better say good-by and get a little sleep." He was slowly relaxing, his taut muscles untensing in a way they hadn't since he'd left Houston. "See you tomorrow evening."

"See you," she agreed softly. "And God bless, Van."

Saturday afternoon Tiffany received another unexpected call. The voice on the other end of the line was low and cultured. "Miss Martin, please."

"This is she."

"Amelia Windsor, here. I'm Van's Gram, in case he's mentioned you to me."

Shock flooded Tiffany. "Y–yes," she stammered. "Has anything happened to him? To his flight?"

"No . . . no . . . dear . . ." The voice seemed a little amused and Tiffany felt herself flushing. "I'm sure Van is fine. I'm calling to invite you to my home next Saturday. It's Van's thirty-first birthday, so I'm having some of his friends out. It will be a very casual affair. Bring a suit if you think the weather's warm enough to venture a swim."

"It sounds delightful." Where had Van's grand-mother heard about her?

Her question was answered almost immediately. "I'm looking forward to meeting you after all Van has told me about you," said the elderly woman. "We must find time for a little woman-to-woman chat. I'm very proud of my grandson, but I'll be the first to admit he's extremely complex."

Tiffany agreed mentally, but refrained from com-mentary. Instead she promised to check with Van about visiting the following Sunday. They ended the conversation on a friendly note and Tiffany hung up the phone, more curious than ever about Van.

Promptly at eight-thirty the next evening, Buck pulled the long sleek limousine to a stop in the church parking lot. Tiffany ignored the admiring glances of her friends, and hurried over to get in, anticipating the moment when she would see Van. Buck spoke in a low voice, "Mr. Windsor has been delayed, so we'll go out to the airport, if you don't mind."

"I hope nothing has gone wrong." Since the deaths of all her family, Tiffany had almost forgotten the pain that comes in thinking something might have hap-pened to a loved one. *Love?* There was that word again—popping into her mind with every thought of Van.

"Just a delay in Amsterdam. He should be in

shortly after we get to the airport. If you'd rather, I could take you home and we could pick you up on our way back."

"No, I'd like to go," assured Tiffany breathlessly.

Two hours passed after they reached the airport and still no plane. The desk clerk evaded inquiries until nearly midnight when he announced the plane should be arriving in less than an hour. Tiffany spent the time trying to concentrate on a book she had with her. It was a losing battle. At length she shoved it back in her purse and prayed silently for Van's safety.

A few minutes before one, the announcement came that the plane was arriving. Tiffany brushed back a strand of hair and hurried with the other travelers to the debarkation gate. The dress she wore was limp and slightly wrinkled, its softly gathered bodice of pale pink cotton flowing over her figure in a way that managed to look charmingly feminine.

The gaunt look on Van's face as he stepped out of the customs room through the swinging doors startled her. He looked around with a frown on his face and she assumed he was expecting Buck to be alone. Too nervous to move, Tiffany waited until his eyes met hers. The grim look was transformed into a welcoming smile as he hurried toward her.

"Tiff," he murmured, swinging his long flight bag over one shoulder.

Unmindful of the crowded room, she swayed toward him and his free arm caught her, pulling her close against him. She moved against him without hesitation, rubbing her head against his chest, feeling such a wave of love that she feared she might be drowning in it. She lifted her head and he gazed down into her eyes for a timeless moment before his mouth descended, moving tantalizingly against her lips with a melting sweetness that filled her with wonder and happiness.

He straightened up with a deep sigh. "I never dreamed you'd be waiting here for me. Where's Buck?"

"He went to get the car." Tiffany didn't protest when his arm slid around her waist as they started down the long hallway to the main lobby. "What made you so late?"

"Some complications. First, our luggage was put on the wrong plane and they had to switch that. Then we started and had to turn around." His grip tightened. "I'm glad to be here."

Buck seemed happy to see his employer as he took the luggage and put it in the rear of the car. As they started the long drive toward Houston, Tiffany leaned into the warm circle of Van's arm, resting her head on his shoulder.

When they neared her place, Van directed Buck to take her home. "It's too late to keep you up, Tiff. You'll have to give me a raincheck on that dinner."

She nodded sleepily, stifling a yawn. "Can't have me falling asleep on the job tomorrow . . . I mean, this morning."

"Take the day off."

What would the others think if Van casually mentioned that Tiffany was too tired to come to work because she'd met him at the airport?

CHAPTER 9

TIFFANY WAS ON TIME the next morning, definitely
tired but determined not to miss work. As usual, Van
was involved all day in matters that demanded his
attention his first day back.

Louise came down shortly before lunch to suggest
they eat together in the lounge. "I brought enough for
both of us. Leftovers from the dinner I served the
pastor and his wife."

"How did that go?" Tiffany felt a little ashamed.
She'd been so caught up in her own world that it
seemed she'd been neglecting Louise lately.

"I enjoyed it immensely. Joss came too, you
know."

"Joss?" For some time Tiffany had suspected that
the relationship between Joss and Louise was not just
the working arrangement that Louise insisted it was.

Louise nodded as they entered the lounge and
selected a table in a far corner. "I thought it might be

good for him to meet a Christian man who's as impressive as our pastor."

"What did Joss think?"

"He didn't say much, but I could tell he was having a great time." Pulling out two pieces of fried chicken, she sighed, "Who knows what Joss is thinking?"

Tiffany let the question go unanswered with only a nod, but she made up her mind to give her friend a little more of her time. "Guess who called me?"

"Who?"

"Van's grandmother."

"Not the *grande dame* herself!"

"What do you mean?"

Louise wiped her fingers on her napkin and reached for some carrot sticks. "I've never met her but from what I've heard she's a haughty old lady . . . expects everyone to bow in her presence. Did you know she raised Van?"

"He said something about it. Do you know anything about his mother?"

"The only time I've ever heard him mention her was when he said the necklace you were wearing had belonged to her. What did Mrs. Windsor want?"

"She invited me to her house for Van's birthday party Saturday. It's an all-day picnic or something. Probably heard some rumors about me after the party that night and wants to take a look for herself."

"It doesn't sound like her. I heard Van laughing about how she ignores any woman he's ever dated . . . just stares through them like they don't exist if he brings them around."

"I haven't mentioned it to Van. Maybe I should just send a polite refusal note . . ."

132

"Coward!" teased Louise. "I'd say it sounds like too much fun to miss."

Van stopped by Tiffany's desk later that afternoon to report on a call from his grandmother. "Thanks for agreeing to go. We'll cut it short if you don't want to waste your whole day."

"Will she have a big birthday cake with thirty-one candles and will we play pin-the-tail-on-the-donkey?" asked Tiffany, keeping her eyes on the broad expanse of chest covered by his crisp white shirt.

Van settled down on the edge of her desk, grinning. "Gram would be scandalized at the very thought. My parties as a kid were these long, formal affairs where I had to dance with all the girls so no one would feel like a wallflower."

"That shows a kind heart."

"How would you know?" His eyes traced the curving contours of her lips. "You've never been a wallflower."

She glanced back down, unable to meet the burning gaze. "How about that raincheck for dinner?" he continued. "Are you free tonight?"

Tiffany knew without looking that Pam had removed her earphone and was listening attentively to their conversation. "Sorry, but I'm busy. I've promised a friend to spend the evening with her."

"'Her'? I think I can handle that. I'm leaving for Atlanta in the morning. How about Friday night?"

She felt miserable. "Friday night I'm giving a bridal shower."

He stood, his jawline taut as if he didn't totally believe her. "Then I'll see you Saturday. It's about a two-hour drive to my grandmother's. Would eight be too early?"

"No, I can make that with no trouble."

"See you then," he said, walking out with that long stride that she enjoyed watching.

Pam made no effort to pretend she hadn't been listening. "Wow, Tiff. You've really got all the men hopping. I thought Van would be furious when he heard about you and Bob Hartman."

Tiffany's heart skipped a beat. "Heard what?" She knew she hadn't mentioned it to anyone.

"This." Pam sauntered over with a smirk on her face and slapped down a clipping from the paper. "Everyone was talking about it in the lounge a few minutes ago. I cut it out for your scrapbook."

Tiffany jerked it up with trembling fingers. It was a blurb from a gossip column. Someone had taken the trouble to underline the incriminating words in black. She read silently, "Who was the gorgeous blonde with financier Bob Hartman at the Inn-on-the-Park the other day? Could she really be Van Windsor's current flame, as Hartman has been telling everyone? If so, we'll all be watching to see the fireworks when Windsor gets back from his latest outrageously successful business trip."

"No!" Tiffany spoke through clenched teeth. "What kind of vulture spends his time spreading rumors like that?" She could have been referring to either Bob or the columnist.

"Is it a lie?" persisted Pam, her beady eyes glittering.

"It's . . ." Tiffany stopped, then added, "Really, it's no one's business, Pam. My opinion of Bob Hartman is dropping lower by the minute. You should be glad he hasn't invited you to any more parties."

Pam shrugged with a faint flush. "I can't understand you, Tiff. You have Van wound around your little finger, but you have to conquer Bob, too. You really fooled me." She glanced back at the switchboard which was lighting up like a Christmas tree.

Tiffany was speechless and heartsick, and Louise did her best to comfort her later that afternoon. "I heard Joss question Van about that column a few minutes ago. Van didn't seem the least bit disturbed. He reminded Joss that you were trying to find out something about the information leak."

The rest of the week Tiffany waited for Van to mention Bob Hartman to her. He didn't. By Friday morning she had made up her mind to tell Van about it herself, but Louise told her Van wouldn't be in that day. "He and Joss are in Baytown to visit that company he's thinking of buying. And guess what! Van invited Joss and me to go to his grandmother's with you two tomorrow. What are you wearing?"

"I haven't made up my mind. Mrs. Windsor stressed wearing something casual, but I'm not sure what she means by that."

"How about a birthday present? Are you getting Van anything?"

"What do you get someone who has everything? I'm at a total loss."

"How about a Bible? You and Joss and I could all go in together and get him one."

"Louise, that's a wonderful idea!" said Tiffany. "Why didn't I think of that? Let's go shopping at noon. I know a place where the owner will engrave the name on the cover while we wait."

Van arrived at Tiffany's apartment a few minutes before eight on Saturday morning. She heard him bounding up the stairs two at a time and had the door open by the time he arrived.

"I'm on my second cup of coffee. Have time for one?" she invited.

He was dressed casually in a thick knitted gray cotton sweater over a pair of darker gray trousers. His jet-black hair was slightly tangled from the brisk breeze and she longed to run her fingers through it.

"Just what I need." His eyes skimmed over her pale green dress with an approving glance. "You look like springtime, Tiff. As fresh and lovely as a spray of apple blossoms."

His words brought a faint pink stain to her cheeks. "Have you ever thought of being a poet?"

He chuckled and followed Tiffany into the compact kitchen.

"By the way, happy birthday," said Tiffany as she poured him a cup of coffee.

"Yep. One year older. How about you, Tiff? How old are you?"

"Twenty-four."

"Such a babe in the woods." There was regret in his voice.

She seized on his genial mood to bring up what was troubling her. "Naïve. Stupid. That's me."

He glanced up in surprise. "In what way?"

"Oh, the Bob Hartman thing. I guess you saw that gossip in the paper."

His lips were set in a grim line as he nodded. "What really happened?"

Relieved to see that he was skeptical about the truth of what he'd read, she told him quickly how Bob had found her in the parking lot with a car that wouldn't start.

"I should have listened to you. He's one of the lowest creatures I've ever met."

Streaks of fire flashed in Van's eyes. "Tell me exactly what he did to you."

"It wasn't that," Tiffany hurried to explain. "What bothered me was what he said. He spent the entire luncheon trying to cut you down. I don't think I've ever seen anyone so intensely jealous."

"Did you learn anything helpful?"

She shook her head with a rueful expression in the golden brown eyes. "He's shrewd, but I'm convinced he's the person who's getting the information. Since he is acquainted with almost everyone at Windsor's, I'm not sure how we can find out who's helping him."

"I know," he sighed. "At least, we're taking much more stringent precautions now against any leaks. I hate to do it, but I'm not even telling Joss every detail."

"You don't suspect *Joss?*" Tiffany was outraged.

"Calm down, Brown Eyes." Van was laughing softly as he reached over and stroked Tiffany's hand. "I trust Joss fully, but this is a protection for him, as well as for the company." Glancing at his watch, he added, "We'd better shove off. Gram considers promptness high on the list of virtues."

As Tiffany went to get her purse, she felt a sense of relief now that she'd discussed Bob Hartman with Van. His equanimity was a surprise. Did it mean that he had reconsidered his peremptory order and decided he had no right to tell her what to do away from work? The thought was oddly depressing.

A sparklingly bright sun cooperated with a light breeze to create a perfect day as the four of them sped

137

along the busy highway and headed toward Mrs. Windsor's country home. Van had explained his grandmother lived in Brenham, a quaint village about fifty miles west of Houston.

Joss was telling Van about a message that had come in shortly before they left so Tiffany leaned back and let her thoughts drift aimlessly. Soon she found herself thinking about Van as a small boy. She smiled inwardly at the picture her imagination conjured up. There's no way he could have been a docile child.

Turning off the main highway onto a narrow country lane, Van turned to Tiffany, "I'd love to know what you're thinking with that mysterious Mona Lisa smile on your lips."

Tiffany fought back a blush. "I was just thinking you don't remind me of someone who grew up on a farm."

The other occupants of the car began laughing. "You're right," conceded Van. "My grandfather retired to a gentleman's ranch after years as a banker. Since his death my grandmother has kept on a foreman and raises a few show horses."

On the highest of the gently rolling grassy green hills stood a stately two-story white wooden home, ornately trimmed with Victorian gingerbread fretwork.

"There's the house," said Van, pride in his voice. "I spent lots of time climbing up those pillars as a kid."

"Your poor grandmother," murmured Tiffany.

"I knew you two would get along."

As they turned into the long circular drive leading to the front of the house, Tiffany saw a brilliant patch of spring flowers. Guests were mingling on the lawn and from a nearby lake bright sun rays exploded into a shimmering iridescence. Walking toward the wide porches that surrounded the house, she caught glimpses of flower-garnished tables laden with an assortment of meats and fruits and fragrant breakfast rolls. Her mouth watered in anticipation.

The murmur of the crowd hushed as Van approached and everyone began calling out birthday congratulations. With a wave of his hand, Van acknowledged the well-wishers, guiding Tiffany through the crowd with a slight pressure on her waist. "We'll go say 'hi' to Gram first," he explained, propelling her up the stairs to the carved wooden front door flanked by stained glass panels.

Once inside the house, Van led Tiffany into a parlor furnished with exquisite Victorian furniture, the kind that would tremble on its fragile carved legs at the sight of a small child. Seated on a striped satin sofa was an elderly woman wearing a pale seafoam-green Georgette dress with a matching picture hat. Her silky white curls framed a serene face.

When she saw Van the lines on her face smoothed out into a welcoming smile. "Van, you're here. And this must be Tiffany. Well, well, how nice to see you, my dear."

Van leaned over and kissed his grandmother's cheek. She reached out and took Tiffany's hands in hers. "She's as beautiful as you described her, Van. After you've eaten, dear, I want Van to bring you back in here so we can have a little time to get acquainted."

Unfriendly? Mrs. Windsor? That must only be another of the rumors Louise had heard. Tiffany had never felt more welcomed by anyone.

"I'd love that," she answered. "You have a beautiful home."

"I love it most for the memories it holds. Now run along, Van, and see about feeding this young woman. Clara has baked your favorite cinnamon rolls, so you must remember to thank her."

Van was grinning as they went back outside. "Why is it that when you go home, you always feel about three years old again?"

"Maybe it's because that's the time parents remember their children as being the sweetest."

For the next two hours they mingled with the guests and gorged themselves on deliciously prepared food. Tiffany gave up trying to remember all the names, concentrating on the few who seemed to be Van's closest friends. She was almost relieved when Van glanced at his watch and said, "Time for you to have that chat with Gram. Promise me you won't believe a word she says about me."

"This is beginning to sound very interesting. Maybe I can add to her store of tales on you."

He pulled her against him with a playful hug. "You wouldn't dare!"

Grandmother Windsor was seated on a small velvet chair in the serenely decorated "morning room" at the back of the house. She indicated Tiffany was to sit opposite her and then shooed Van out of the room. As soon as he left she leaned forward, and eyed Tiffany thoughtfully. Her eyes were kind, yet quizzical. "What do you really think of my grandson?" she asked at length.

Tiffany managed a slight smile. "He's . . . he's . . . well . . . ." She paused, shrugging her shoulders helplessly.

"Dynamic. Forceful. Charming." Mrs. Windsor supplied the adjectives. "Perhaps a little stubborn and selfish? She smiled understandingly and patted Tiffany's hand. "I can see the truth in your eyes, my dear. You love him, don't you?"

Tiffany was completely speechless for a moment and she felt her face beginning to burn. Under the intent gaze of Van's grandmother she found herself nodding her head. The regal face relaxed into a smile.

"That's good. He may not be too easy to live with; I'm afraid he was spoiled as a child. He missed his mother so much when he arrived here I couldn't bring myself to enforce much discipline." Peering over at Tiffany, she said, "I can see he hasn't told you much about his mother. It's a very painful subject for him, and he keeps it all bottled up inside."

Tiffany was still trying to recover from her shock. *Van's Gram thinks I'm going to marry him!* she realized. Who had told her such a tale? And what had possessed Tiffany to admit she loved him? Forcing herself to concentrate on the elderly woman's words, she heard her say, "I would not discuss Van's mother as idle gossip, but I think you need to know why Van has such a difficult time trusting any woman. You see, his father, my only child, died when Van was an infant. His mother was a beautiful English actress, talented, ambitious, but totally unsuited to motherhood. She brought Van to me when he was four, telling the child she was only leaving him for a few days. He grieved over her for weeks. Just as he began to settle down, she returned and started the cycle all over again."

Tiffany murmured sympathy and Mrs. Windsor nodded before continuing, "Yes, it was tragic. He loved his mother so dearly—who wouldn't? She was an exotic creature, dressed in beautiful clothes, smelling like a bouquet of flowers, and making wild and extravagant promises. This continued for several years until she finally died of pneumonia when Van was nine. Her death almost devastated Van. The end of all his dreams.''

"But why did you let her keep coming back?''

"I asked myself that question. I'd like to think it was because I was too soft-hearted. But the truth is I kept hoping the woman would settle down and take him back. I was so busy with my own life I didn't have any inclination to rear another son.''

Tiffany sat still, absorbing this new view of Van. So much of the enigma surrounding the man was becoming clear. Deserted by his mother, aware he was an intrusion in his grandmother's life—no wonder he was so fiercely independent now. could he ever allow himself to trust any woman's love?

Mrs. Windsor seemed to sense Tiffany's confusion. "Well, enough of that,'' she said briskly. "Now tell me about yourself, dear. I hope we'll be friends.''

A maid interrupted a short time later, announcing the arrival of another guest and Tiffany excused herself, glad to escape the quizzical eyes of the elderly woman. She knew she should have made it plain there was nothing serious between Van and herself, but she couldn't bring herself to destroy his grandmother's happy illusions. *Let Van straighten that out*, Tiffany decided.

Most of the guests had gathered around the sparkling waters of a large swimming pool, but few were brave enough to venture into the cold water. Van was surrounded by several skimpily clad beauties and

Tiffany tried to slip over to the sidelines without being noticed. But he caught sight of her almost instantly and made his way over.

"What happened between you and Gram?"

Tiffany grinned. "I'll never tell."

He pulled her against him, kissing her on the nose. "Wait until I get you alone. I'll tickle it out of you."

Enjoying his nearness and the faint aroma of a spicy masculine scent, Tiffany leaned against him. "If you do, I'll squeal to your grandmother."

"Oh, so it's like that, is it?" His arms were tightening around her when someone bumped into them, splattering water over their clothes.

Van groaned irritably and glared at a man who was weaving past them. "Watch where you're going, buddy!" Van told him, lightly brushing the droplets from Tiffany's dress. "Do you need a towel?"

"No . . . uh," Tiffany mumbled, her heart racing at the inadvertent caress.

Van laughed softly and warmth rushed from Tiffany's throat to her cheeks. She tried to think of a light remark to show Van she wasn't reacting to his slightest touch, but not one coherent thought came to mind.

Later that afternoon Mrs. Windsor made her appearance, and a trolley of gifts was rolled out by a uniformed maid. Van seemed embarrassed, muttering his displeasure under his breath, but he went through the motions of opening the lavishly wrapped gifts with a show of appreciation. Most were the type of expensive masculine items found in the sleek mail-order catalogs that Tiffany loved to peruse. She suspected Van had little use for any of them.

143

Louise nudged her, pointing to their own gift. "I can't wait for him to open ours!"

Tiffany was a little less certain how she felt. Would the gift of a Bible embarrass Van in front of his sophisticated friends? Tossing her head, she forced such cowardly thoughts from her mind.

Theirs was one of the last he reached for, and it seemed to take Van forever to unwrap the box. When he lifted the lid and took out the Bible, Tiffany held her breath.

A man about his age, slightly under the influence of all the drinks that had been served, began laughing. "What's this, Van? Someone think you need a little reforming?"

Van's laugh rang out. "It wouldn't hurt." Glancing over at Tiffany, Joss, and Louise, he said, "Thanks. I hate to admit it, but I don't have one of these in my home." He laid it aside and made short work of the last few packages.

The only flaw in an otherwise perfect day came about an hour before they left. It was twilight and the maids were clearing off the evening meal that had been served a few hours earlier. Tiffany was sitting beside Van, listening as a married couple were telling him about their plans to open a restaurant in Brenham. Her eyes were drifting downward and she leaned against Van, enjoying the feel of his lithe, muscular body and the arm wrapped around her.

She was startled into alertness by the sound of Bob Hartman's voice. "Happy birthday and all that sort of nonsense, Van. Sorry to be so late."

Van glanced over his shoulder. "Gram is the one who'll expect your apologies. She's in the parlor."

144

"Oh, the queen is greeting her subjects?" Bob's voice was laced with sarcasm.

Van only nodded but Tiffany felt his arm tighten around her. "Ah, the beautiful Miss Martin," continued Bob, in a much louder voice than was necessary. "Did she tell you about our tête-à-tête at the Inn while you were out of the country?"

"Any special reason she should?" returned Van. "Bob, have you met Aaron and Julie Sorenson? They're thinking about opening a restaurant in the old Grimes house in Brenham. Maybe you'll lend them your sage advice." Van stood, helping Tiffany to her feet. "Let's go inside and tell Gram good-by."

"Yes, let's," Tiffany said eagerly. Why had she given Bob this chance to make such an intimate remark in front of Van's friends?

Van was careful not to mention Bob as they strolled toward the stately house together but Tiffany sensed a tenseness in him that he seemed determined to hide. She didn't like the way she was beginning to be able to guess what he was thinking. It made her too vulnerable, almost as if there were a bond between them. Thinking that way, she knew, was a quick one-way ticket to misery.

CHAPTER 10

JOSS WAS RED-FACED and angry as the four of them reached the car a few minutes later. "Did you hear that Allen? He's telling everyone that he's thinking of buying into the solar power consortium—the one you've been negotiating with. If I can can ever get my hands on the person who's giving that guy our secrets . . ."

"Don't let it get to you," said Van. "The only way he's going to know what I'm bidding is if he's a mind reader. I'm not even writing it on paper for my own eyes."

"What a mess!" groaned Louise. "To think there's a traitor in our ranks."

Van sounded grim. "It bothers me every time I walk through the offices. Anyone come up with any clues yet?"

"I lean toward Dave Allredge," stated Louise matter-of-factly.

"Why? What's the motive? Neither Bob nor his dad can offer Dave a better deal than I'm giving him."

"Pam's *my* bet," said Joss.

"What's *her* motive?" defended Tiffany. "Anyway, I mentioned Pam's name to Bob the day I had lunch with him, and he had to ask who she was. I don't think she's guilty."

"Then that leaves Buck, and I can't bring myself to doubt his loyalty." With a sudden gesture of dismissal, Van said, "Hey, folks. This is my birthday. Can't we think of something more pleasant to discuss?"

Tiffany had enjoyed herself so thoroughly she was reluctant to see the day end as she and Van stopped in front of her apartment complex. "Think you could fix some more of that good coffee?" Van asked.

"Love to."

She ignored the fluttering of her heart as she prepared two steaming mugs. They carried them into the living area and Van settled down beside her on the sofa. "Have a good time today?" he asked.

"Wonderful! At first I felt in such awe of your grandmother, but she graciously set me at ease."

"I could tell she loved you." He set down his cup and slipped an arm over her shoulder, his fingers curving around her arm. "There's something about you the Windsors can't resist."

She hesitated, but he drew her toward him, removing her mug and placing it on the coffee table. A warm feeling of contentment surged through Tiffany and she rested against his broad chest, listening to the beat of his heart. As his lean fingers closed over her neck, he moved even closer, lowering his head until his firm mouth brushed hers. He raised his head slightly, his

147

darkening eyes wandering over her face and coming to rest on her gaze for a heart-stopping moment.

Perhaps she could blame it on being exhausted or perhaps it was only that everything that day had seemed to be casting a spell on her bemused senses, but Tiffany offered no resistance when Van's lips reached hers once more. His warm mouth covered her own softly parted lips in a light, gentle kiss, and she melted against him, trusting herself to his tender caresses.

His mouth began to move on hers, murmuring barely distinguishable words of endearment. Tiffany went limp in his arms. She clutched his shoulders with both hands, reveling in his clean fresh scent and the warmth of his strong masculine frame.

When he paused and looked at her wonderingly, she tried to dredge up the strength to move away, but she couldn't. At the moment it seemed only that this was what she had been lacking all her life—this, the intimacy she'd always dreamed of. That she and Van were meant for each other, body, soul, mind, and spirit. Surely, they had been brought together for some purpose, something more than a brief encounter. . . .

Even as Van's desire reached a fever pitch of urgency, an inner voice was cautioning him: *Slow down. There's so much more to this woman than a beautiful body. She has strength and goodness and the kind of love to offer that you never knew existed.*

He didn't want to cheapen that purity and virtue by using his expertise to enflame her senses, making her forget momentarily all the things that combined to make her the person he admired so deeply. Sitting there, drinking deeply of the fragrance of her soft, warm skin and the long, silky strands of her thick hair, sampling the tastes and textures of her feminine lips, he realized suddenly that he would never be satisfied with less than total commitment from Tiffany.

The thought staggered him. What was he thinking? Marriage? He felt almost physically ill. Marriage wasn't on his agenda. He had vowed as a child he'd never give *any* woman power over him again. Not even someone as honest and trustworthy as this woman.

Abruptly he wrenched himself away. "Tiffany . . . my sweet, sweet Tiffany," he murmured, his gaze sliding away from the delicate features filled with a returning adoration.

Tiffany read his look accurately, shame coursing through her as she realized she had given away her yearning and love for Van. She moved away, straightening her skirt and reaching with shaky hands for the coffee cup. The tepid liquid sent a shiver through her as she took a gulp.

"Tiff . . ." Van's voice sounded anguished.

Not pity. She could stand anything but pity from Van.

"Sorry if I fell apart like that," she said in what she hoped was a casual voice. "I guess I'm not used to such expertise."

His voice was gruff and angry. "Stop it. It's my fault I let that get out of hand. You know how much I want you, but . . ."

She placed a finger over his lips lightly. "I understand completely, Van, and thank you for respecting my beliefs. You've finally convinced me that all those war stories about how you discard women as careless-

149

ly as some men do their dirty socks were part of your false image."

His slow smile almost melted her into a fiery puddle. "If only one of us were different, Tiff. We could have . . ."

"Yes," she said, inhaling deeply. "But it's good we both recognize how different we are. Still, I hope we can be friends."

"I don't know. Mere friendship doesn't seem much of a possibility between us." He rose to his feet with slow determination.

He couldn't just leave . . . taking such a vital part of herself with him, she thought wildly. She took a deep breath and forced herself to stand beside him, smoothing down her flowing skirt with quick, nervous strokes. She vowed she'd be as cool and composed as he appeared to be. At least on the outside, she added ruefully. Why try to fool herself?

She was pleased with the serene note she injected into her voice when they walked to the door. "Thanks for a wonderful day, Van. Let me know your grandmother's address so I can drop her a note."

Her throat tightened as she mentioned his grandmother. The elderly woman would wonder what had happened between her grandson and Tiffany. She'd made it plain enough that she was banking on Tiffany to break down Van's wall of resistance to women. Now, she'd realize what a futile wish that had been.

Van leaned over and brushed his lips against Tiffany's cheek when they reached the door. Without a backward glance he went out the door and she closed it behind him, leaning against it and letting the tears flow unchecked. After several minutes she choked back the sobs, ignoring the deep ache inside her and went into the bath, turning on the shower before stripping off her clothes.

You knew all along Van Windsor wasn't for you, she berated herself. He had never made any pretense of being a Christian. She had only herself to blame for thinking about him, accepting his invitations to go places with him, dreaming about him at night.

Well, maybe you couldn't control those wild, crazy dreams about Van, she conceded ruefully, stepping under the hard, cleansing spray of the warm water. *But how about God's promise that things work together for good in the lives of those who love Him?* She was so busy feeling sorry for herself she hadn't even thought of that. There was a purpose for her meeting Van, for caring for him this way. Maybe she'd never know all the answers, but she intended to pray for him. In some small way, he would always be a part of her life.

Van mentally cursed himself as he drove home. What had that nobility scene been about? He'd had in his arms a warm, willing woman whose slightest touch drove him insane, and *he'd* been the one to call a halt. What made him think he knew what was best for Tiffany? If she felt anything like he did, she was miserable right now. What could giving a little pleasure to each other have mattered all that much?

But what about afterwards? that relentless inner voice reminded him. *She would have wanted vows of trust and faithfulness, love and marriage. Could you have faced the look of betrayal on her face when you broke with her?* Sure, it would have forced her to grow up, face what life was really about, make her realize she wasn't ever going to find any man worthy of her love, but he knew he wanted no part in administering that lesson.

Thoroughly disgusted with himself for the strange thoughts assailing him, he veered into the drive in front of his condominium, ordering the doorman to see that someone delivered the packages in the trunk of his car to his apartment. "Yes sir," returned the man. "Right away, sir."

Still muttering over the man's meek obeisance, Van strode into his condo a few minutes later. A light shone brightly from the kitchen and he called out, "Is that you, Mrs. Duncan?"

Dressed in a bright blue robe that gave her a cheery look, the housekeeper stepped into the doorway. "Yes, sir. Did you need anything, sir?"

"For heaven's sake!" he snapped. "You're not on duty twenty-four hours a day!"

"But I don't mind . . ."

"You ought to." Van joined her in the kitchen. "Don't pay any attention to me. Any messages?"

"I put them on the desk in your study. None were urgent." She peered at him with a worried expression. "Would you like a little warm milk? I was just fixing myself a cup."

Van chuckled. "No, thanks. But maybe a little warm talk."

"How was Mrs. Windsor, sir?"

He sat down across from her. "She looked good."

"I'm sure she was pleased to meet Miss Martin." Her eyes held the look of a cat licking cream.

"So it was *you*." Van smiled again. "I knew someone besides me had been bragging about Tiffany to Gram."

"Well, she did ask my opinion."

"It must have been good."

"Oh, the best. I know a fine young woman when I meet one."

"I agree entirely." Van rose restlessly and the doorbell at the rear of the apartment sounded.

Mrs. Duncan's hand flew to her throat. "Who would be using the delivery elevator this late?"

"My birthday presents," explained Van, whipping open the door. After tipping the delivery man generously, he rummaged through the sacks, holding out several expensive presents for Mrs. Duncan to admire.

With a sudden gesture he held up the Bible. "It will please you to know that Miss Martin gave me this for my birthday. Now, have you ever heard of a more perfect young woman?"

Mrs. Duncan's eyes rounded in surprise over the heavy sarcasm in his voice. "That is a mite unusual," she conceded nervously.

Van carried it over to the table and sat back down, flipping through it for several minutes. "Do you know where Galatians is?" he asked suddenly.

"It's one of the Apostle Paul's epistles." Mrs. Duncan felt at a loss; she hadn't attended church in all the years since her husband had died. "In the New Testament. There's sure to be a table of contents in the front."

"Oh." Van turned to the front, located the name and then turned to the correct page. "Galatians 3:26: 'For you are all the children of God by faith in Christ Jesus.' Do you know what that means?" he demanded.

"I think so. It means God is everyone's Heavenly Father."

"Wrong. Tiffany says it's much more personal than that. It's an individual choice we have to make. We have to decide if we want to believe God, to accept that we can never be good enough to meet His standards. Then we have to believe that He sent His Son, the Lord Jesus Christ, to die in our place. Then we're born into God's family." Van flipped the Bible shut with a bang. "Do you know some of those five-year-old children Tiffany was teaching knew more than I did about God, Mrs. Duncan?"

"No . . . I can't imagine . . ." Her hands fluttered nervously.

Van rose and patted her cheek. "You must think I'm a little crazy tonight. Maybe what I need is a good night's sleep."

"Yes, it *is* late."

Van stayed awake for hours, reading and rereading chapters in the Bible. It was nearly dawn before he bowed his head and asked God to accept him as a member of His family. When he finally closed his eyes, he slept soundly, resting in the firm assurance that his prayer had been both heard and answered.

When he awoke the next morning, Van grabbed up the receiver to call Tiffany before noting the time on the clock. Nearly eleven! She'd already be at church. After a quick shower and shave, he decided to drive over to her apartment and be waiting when she came home.

Twelve came and went and still no Tiffany. Maybe she was at Louise's, he decided. When he reached her apartment, Louise met him the door. "Van! Come on in and have a bite of lunch. I was just wishing I had someone to talk to."

He tried to hide his disappointment. "Sorry, but I have to run. Any idea where Tiffany is?"

"In Woodville. She called at the crack of dawn and told me she was going to her hometown to attend church this morning. Sounded a little homesick."

"Did she say when she'd be back?"

"Not until late. I promised to help out in the teen class for her this evening. If you really need to talk to her, I might be able to locate the number of one of her friends. . . ."

"No, I'll see her tomorrow. Thanks, anyway."

Joss called shortly after he returned home. "The solar power deal is on. I've got you a reservation to fly out to Zurich tonight and the negotiations will take place at a secret rendezvous near there."

"Tonight?" Van's need to see Tiffany was like a hollow ache.

"I thought you'd be shouting over the news. It means you've beat out Hartman and his old man."

"Oh, I am, I am," assured Van. "Give me the details of the flight, and I'll get ready right away." Maybe this was better after all, Van conceded. It would give him more time to read his Bible and sort through his feelings before trying to explain them to Tiffany.

The next morning, when Tiffany learned about Van's sudden trip, she tried convincing herself she was glad he was out of the country. It gave her an opportunity to accept the fact that she had to stop thinking about him so much. By the time he got back, she was determined to see him as nothing more than an excellent boss who lived in another world.

Pam was in a particularly difficult mood that week,

sitting morosely at her desk with a long face, ready to snarl at anyone who crossed her. When Tiffany tried asking her what was bothering her, she burst into tears and ran to the ladies room. Louise, in her role as office manager, called her in and explained that her behavior would have to improve or she would be asked to find another job. After that, Pam attempted to be more cheerful.

On Thursday morning, her voice quavered as she greeted a guest and Tiffany swirled in her desk to get a better view of him. It was Bob Hartman. He caught a glimpse of Tiffany and brushed past Pam's desk.

"Just the woman I was looking for. I've come with an olive branch, Tiff. How about having lunch with me while I explain why I'm feeling as low as a snake about how I treated you?"

"Apology accepted. But lunch is definitely out." Tiffany turned back to her computer.

"Aw, Tiff. Don't be like that. I can't get you out of my mind." When Tiffany didn't answer he turned back to Pam. "How about it, Pam, old girl. Can you talk this hard-hearted beauty into giving me another chance?"

"Get out of here," hissed Pam in a menacing tone that made Tiffany start in surprise. "I hate you, Bob Hartman! I hate everything about you! Get out. . . ." Her words were swallowed by choking sobs.

"Do you think I care what a little mouse like you thinks?" He was almost laughing.

"You will care when I tell Van what you made me do."

"Made you do? I don't have the slightest idea what you're talking about." He shrugged and cocked his head in Tiffany's direction. "Ever thought about having this girl's head checked? I think she's having a nervous breakdown."

When Pam jumped from her chair and started toward him with fire in her eye, Tiffany quickly dialed Joss. "Come quick. We've got a problem in the outer office."

Bob glanced from Pam to Tiffany and made a hasty retreat to the door. "What a bunch of crazies Windsor's got working for him," he muttered on his way out.

By the time Joss reached the outer office, Pam had dissolved into tears. Joss looked at her in disgust. "What's this all about? You better pull yourself together, Pam."

"That's enough, Joss," said Tiffany, putting her arms around Pam. "I'm afraid you missed the action. Bob Hartman came in here and insulted her."

Joss's frown cleared and was replaced by anger. "If he ever sets foot in here again, he's going to regret it. Sorry I blew off like that, Pam," he added gruffly. "Are you going to be OK?"

"Yes, I think so."

"Why don't you have Louise get her a replacement from the mail room? Pam and I'll go over to my apartment and have lunch while she calms down." Tiffany was determined to get to the bottom of this altercation between Bob and Pam.

"Good idea. Do you need a ride?"

"No, we're in good shape." Tiffany got her purse and held on to Pam's arm as they left the office together. Once in her apartment, she fixed the young girl a glass of iced tea and sat down on the sofa beside her.

"Thanks for defending me to Joss," said Pam.

"Louise already warned me that if I fell apart again, I'd have to be replaced."

"She's right. A front-office receptionist has to be calm and poised—even in the most trying circumstances," agreed Tiffany. "Maybe you're getting tired of that job. Have you ever thought about training for something else?"

"I've got to get away," nodded Pam, still sniffing from her recent crying jag. "It isn't the job, though. It's Bob."

"Forget him. I know what it feels like to have him tell a bunch of lies."

Pam concentrated on her glass of tea. "He wasn't lying," she mumbled.

Tiffany waited to make certain she had understood her correctly. "What do you mean?"

"Are you going to tell Van?"

"I'll have to think about it." She didn't intend making any promises she couldn't keep.

Pam began sobbing again. "Oh, it's terrible, Tiff. I honestly didn't know what I was doing at first. Bob asked me to a couple of his parties and started acting like he really cared for me."

"And?" Tiffany probed gently.

"I thought all my dreams had come true. At last a handsome, rich man was in love with me. I was such a fool."

"How?"

Pam's voice was barely above a whisper. "I didn't see how it could hurt Van to help Bob just a little. He told me that companies do this all time, that he'd caught a guy working for him who was on Van's payroll, too. So, I just watched Louise open the safe and memorized the combination." She glanced up,

"I've got this thing about numbers. Once I see them, I never forget them. So then I watched for an opportunity to slip in and get out the reports. All Bob wanted were the numbers written on the front. I didn't even read the reports."

Tiffany exhaled deeply, feeling Pam's betrayal deep inside her. "What happened?"

"Bob was furious when I got sick and couldn't get in the safe anymore. That was about the time Barry died. Afterwards I learned the new combination and I thought everything was going to be great between us. Then, when Louise quit writing numbers on the reports . . ." She paused. "Did he try to get *you* to help him?"

"He might have, but we didn't get along from the first. The reason I went out to lunch with him was because Van suspected Bob."

Pam's eyes flew open wider. "Then Van knows? What will he do to me? Am I in serious trouble?"

"I honestly don't know, but I think you need to tell Van."

"I can't. I'm afraid," moaned Pam.

"If you tell him, it'll go much easier, Pam. Van's a kind man."

"I don't know . . . I don't know what to do." She began crying again.

"Of course you do. You'll do what's right," said Tiffany with more conviction than she was feeling. "Now go wash your face while I fix us some sandwiches. You're going to find out that telling the truth makes you feel much better."

Pam came back in a few minutes, much calmer. "I do feel better," she admitted. "When is Van due back? I don't think I can stand it until I've confessed."

"I'm not sure when he'll be back. Why don't we talk to Louise this afternoon and she'll think of the best way to handle it. If you tell her what you told me, she'll be fair."

"Oh, Tiff, do you really think so? You don't know how much I appreciate this. I'll work the rest of my life to make it up . . ."

Tiffany smiled over the extravagant promises. It was out of her hands now; she'd have to live with whatever decision Van made regarding Pam. Why was she so certain that he'd be gentle and understanding with the troubled young girl?

Louise's face took on a grim look as Pam recited her treachery later that afternoon, but she relented, admitting that she could understand how tempting Bob Hartman must have made his requests for help. "Are you certain you won't fall for him again?" she demanded.

"Never!" said Pam. "I've learned my lesson."

"Then let's leave it at that for now. There's no need to mention it to Joss until Van gets back."

"When will that be?" asked Tiffany eagerly.

"Joss says Van is supposed to call tomorrow and let us know when his flight is scheduled."

"Thank you! Thank you!" Pam was almost hysterical in her relief over having the truth known at last.

Van called Tiffany late that evening. The sound of his voice sent a wave of longing through her. "Where are you, Van?"

"Near Zurich. I've been wanting to call you, but we all agreed to a secret meeting."

"Did everything turn out right for you?"

"Yes. More than you'll know, Tiff. Something happened to me the night before I left Houston."

Me, too, thought Tiffany ruefully. "Was it good, Van?"

"The best. I joined your team."

"My team?"

"Christians versus lions."

"Van!" He couldn't possibly mean what she was thinking.

He was laughing. "Yes, I mean it. I was so mad at myself when I left you that night. Walking away from the most beautiful, desirable woman in the world. I kicked myself the whole way home. Then when I got there, I found the Bible you gave me."

"And?" She was breathless in anticipation.

"It took me a little while, but I found the verse you taught the little angels in your class the other morning."

Her mind went blank a moment, but he added, "For you are all the children of God through faith in Christ Jesus. I decided I needed to be a member of that family."

"And you believed. . . ."

"That Christ died for my sins? Right! I read the Gospel of John until almost dawn. I don't see how anyone could read that book through and not make the right decision."

"Van . . ." she murmured softly, scarcely aware that tears of happiness were streaming down her face.

"Are you still there?" he asked after a pause.

"Yes . . . oh, yes. I'm so happy . . ."

161

"That you're crying?" He was chuckling softly.

"Not anymore."

"We've got a lot to talk about when I get back, Tiff."

"Yes, Van! Yes! When?"

"Saturday. I don't have a reservation yet, but I'll call as soon as I get in. Can I see you?"

"Try staying away!"

His low, satisfied laugh was filled with exciting promises.

All day Friday Tiffany could hardly contain the joy she was feeling. She decided not to mention Van's call to Louise. Let him share his good news with others in his own way when he was ready. For now, she was satisfied just knowing what his words implied. Not that she intended fooling herself that this meant Van was in love with her. No, she didn't dare allow herself to think that. But given time, who knew what might happen? Of one thing she was certain—she would never again try to limit God or the power of His Word.

Friday evening Tiffany cleaned her apartment. By the time she was finished, she was almost too tired to eat. After resting in front of the television set for almost an hour, she flipped it off and went into the kitchen. Her stomach was jumpy with anticipation every time she thought of seeing Van again, but she forced herself to heat a can of soup and eat most of it. Afterward, she took a shower and was preparing for bed when the doorbell rang. For a moment her heart skipped a beat. Could Van possibly be back earlier than anticipated?

"Van?" she called out, shrugging into a robe.

162

"Yes." The voice was muffled and, without thinking, she flung open the door, a welcoming smile on her face.

Bob Hartman stood there, a lopsided grin on his face. "Hi, babe. Sorry to disappoint you, but it's not lover boy." His words were slightly slurred.

She attempted to slam the door but his foot snaked out, preventing it from closing, and he pushed past her. "You've got to let me use your phone. I had a little wreck . . . down the street . . . can't let the police . . ." His words were almost unintelligible.

"Are you hurt?" she asked grudgingly, looking for any signs of injury.

"I'll live. Where's your phone?"

"In the bedroom, but you'll have to wait outside as soon as you've made your call."

"Don't worry; I didn't expect you to help." He disappeared into the bedroom and Tiffany paced the floor, tempted to leave the door open. When she began shivering from the cool, damp air, she closed the door as quietly as possible.

Straining to hear, she listened to Bob's voice but couldn't make out the words. Hearing the slam of the receiver, she breathed a sign of relief and then there was another knock at the door.

"Who's there?" she called out nervously.

"Joss."

She threw open the door. "Joss, am I ever glad to see you. Bob Hartman . . ."

"Darling, when you are coming to bed?" Bob's voice sounded, clear and commanding, without any trace of his former fuzziness.

"Yes?" Joss gave her a cynical sneer.

"You don't understand. Bob pushed his way past

me tonight. He said he'd been in an accident and needed to use my phone." She stopped talking as Bob strolled into the living room, wearing only a pair of trousers.

"You too, Joss? Seems like Tiffany is a busy lady." he drawled.

"Get out of here," said Tiffany as soon as she had recovered her voice.

Joss surveyed the scene and then said calmly. "You heard the lady. She said to get out."

Bob shrugged. "Okay, I'm leaving. She's all yours." He reemerged from the bedroom minutes later, fully dressed and left without a word.

"What's that all about?" asked Joss when they were alone.

"I've already told you. What are you doing here?"

"I got a call about an hour ago. Told me I'd learn something interesting the boss would want to know about if I came by here at this time."

"Why, that . . . that . . ." Her vocabulary didn't include a word vile enough to describe Bob Hartman.

"It wasn't Hartman. It was a woman."

"He put her up to it."

Joss seemed unconvinced. "It's late. Why would you let him in?"

Tiffany flared in anger. "If you don't believe me, that's your business, but I'm telling the truth."

Joss lowered his eyes. "I want to believe you, Tiff, but Van's got to know about this since it concerns the company."

"Tell him!" said Tiffany, madder than she ever remembered being in her whole life. "He'll trust me. I know he will." She slammed the door behind Joss after he had backed out.

Minutes later she sat down on the sofa, trembling with shock. Was it expecting too much of Van to think he could trust her?

She remembered what his grandmother had told her, and tears misted her eyes as she recalled the story of his mother's betrayal. Now he was being presented what appeared to be indisputable proof of another woman's untrustworthiness. Hers.

She bowed her head and rested it in her hands, crying softly and murmuring a prayer that Van would believe she would never betray him. Surely there was some way she could explain to him, some way to make him see that the faith she had expounded to him and he had come to accept was vital and working in her own life.

But she knew it wasn't going to be easy for Van. He was too wary, still too scarred to brush this aside easily. He had known Joss for years, and he trusted him. How could she expect him to take her word over his friend's?

The question haunted her throughout a long, almost sleepless night.

CHAPTER 11

TIFFANY CALLED LOUISE as soon as she awoke the next morning. Her friend was completely sympathetic when she heard the story.

"I can't believe Joss acted like that," she kept repeating.

"It *did* look bad," Tiffany admitted.

"But why would he take the word of some anonymous caller and sneak by your apartment that way? I'm ashamed of him."

"You forget we didn't tell him about Pam's part in the information leak. He was still checking out every clue he heard about."

"Well, *you* can defend him if you want to, but *I* intend to give him a piece of my mind when I see him. If he goes running to Van with that tall tale . . ." She didn't need to finish the sentence.

"I know," moaned Tiffany. "If only I hadn't opened that door without taking a peek out the window. Van warned me once not to open my door to strangers."

"Van will believe you." Louise's voice was firm. "He's due in this afternoon. Why don't you meet him at the airport and tell your side before Joss gets to him?"

Tiffany was tempted but decided against it. Van would be too exhausted after his busy schedule to be greeted at the airport by a woman trying to justify herself. No, it didn't seem fair. She hoped Joss would be equally understanding.

"No, I don't think so. I think I'll run by Pam's house this morning. I'm a little worried about her. She has been close to the edge these last few weeks."

"I'll go with you," declared Louise. "We'll talk to her a little more and get some exact details about what information she gave Bob. I imagine she'll be so hysterical with Van that she won't be able to remember a thing!"

Tiffany agreed, laughing, and then went to fix herself a bowl of cereal before Louise came by. Today everything seemed much brighter. Of course, Van would believe her. He had to.

Pam's eyes were red-rimmed and puffy when she opened the door, but she seemed pleased to see Tiffany and Louise. Her apartment was cluttered, newspapers and clothes draped haphazardly over the backs of chairs. After gathering up a handful, she went into the kitchen and filled a kettle with water.

"Bob Hartman called last night," she said in a lifeless voice.

"What did he want?" Had he coerced Pam into calling Joss?

"Said to tell you, Tiff, that he had evened the score. I couldn't understand everything, but it sounded like he thought he'd gotten you in a lot of trouble with Van. I'm sorry."

"I can handle it," said Tiffany. "Maybe while we drink our tea, you'll tell us all you can remember about the information Bob got from you. It will help Van if he knows."

Pam burst into tears and sank down in a chair, leaving Tiffany to finish pouring the tea. "I'm so ashamed of myself. I still can't believe I thought I had a chance with Bob—that I'd even *want* one. He's a real jerk!"

"Calm down and start talking," said Louise. "If you want to help yourself out of this mess, you'll tell everything you can remember. But keep it truthful."

"I will. I promise."

Louise took rapid notes as Pam talked, her face growing grimmer with each new revelation. "On the surface none of these pieces of information looked important," she said to Pam. "But altogether, you've cost Van a lot of money."

"What will he do?"

"I honestly don't know," said Louise, "But your only chance for leniency is to face up to him. If you try to run away, you'll be in more trouble than you can handle."

"I won't run away. When can I see him?"

"I'll check with Joss." She crossed to the phone. After a brief conversation she returned. "Joss is on his way over here. I think he needs to hear some of this from you, Pam."

"He'll be *furious*," moaned Pam.

While they waited, Tiffany encouraged Pam to

straighten up her apartment. "I'll do these dishes in the sink while you hang up the clothes."

"Good idea," said Louise, getting a plastic trash bag from the cabinet and stuffing it with the old papers.

Joss ignored Tiffany as she let him in the door, but spotted Pam and immediately began his interrogation.

Louise broke in, "I have notes here of everything and I'll type them up this afternoon before Van arrives. I just wanted you to know that Tiffany is the one who found out the truth from Pam."

Joss glanced over at Tiffany, his eyes still showing skepticism. "When did this happen?"

"Thursday morning . . ."

His face flushed an angry red. "And you women waited until *now* to tell me?"

"That was my decision," said Louise. "Tell him briefly, Pam, that you're the one who told Bob Hartman the numbers on the reports."

"I'm guilty, Joss," said Pam. "I let Bob trick me."

"All you women seem to be having some trouble in that department," accused Joss gruffly.

"What will Van do?"

"I never try reading his mind," said Joss.

Louise dropped Tiffany off at her apartment on her way home, and the rest of the afternoon loomed ominously before her. She couldn't sit by the phone, waiting breathlessly to see if Van was going to call her. On the other hand, what if he tried and she wasn't home?

At length she compromised, going next door and offering to care for the neighbor's baby girl while they went for a drive. With the child in her arms, Tiffany went back to her own apartment and played with her until she fell asleep. When the parents returned, the phone was still silent.

As the afternoon shadows lengthened, Tiffany began to face the fact that Van had not rushed to the phone to call her. Desperate to hear from him, she called Mrs. Duncan and asked if he had returned.

"Yes, Miss Martin, he did. Came in about an hour ago with Joss and then they went out again. Shall I give him a message when he comes back?"

"No," said Tiffany dully. Van must have believed Joss.

When her phone did ring, she almost tripped in her haste to answer it. The caller was Louise.

"How about going out to dinner with me tonight? A little Mexican food ought to liven us up."

Tea and sympathy? Was that what Louise was offering. It was better than a long evening alone, Tiffany decided.

"Thanks. Where shall I meet you?"

"I'll come by. And dress up in your best, Tiff. Times like this you have to shine."

Tiffany laughed shakily but agreed. She was wearing the rose silk Van had admired once, with a single strand of pearls nestling around her neck, when she heard Louise at the door. The older woman scrutinized Tiffany from head to toe, patting several strands of hair into place.

"You'll do," she said at length.

"Thanks," said Tiffany huskily. "I didn't know you were so particular about how your friends dressed."

Louise flushed. "I only meant that I'm glad to see you're not moaning over what happened last night. Pam's crying jag almost got me down."

"Nothing to worry about here," bluffed Tiffany, leading the way downstairs. To her surprise, Joss's car was parked in front. He was sitting in the driver's seat. She turned accusingly on Louise, "You didn't mention . . ."

"We need a crowd to cheer us up tonight," explained Louise with an engaging grin. Tiffany felt like throttling her.

Joss's earlier grim mood had vanished. He welcomed Tiffany with a friendly greeting. She longed to ask him about Van. Had Joss told him about finding Bob in her apartment? If so, what had he said? The questions refused to come out.

Close on the heels of those thoughts came an equally depressing one. What if this whole idea of dinner out tonight was Van's idea? Worse still, what if Joss and Louise were being paid overtime to make certain Tiffany didn't sit by her phone waiting for the call he had promised? After several moments she forced herself to join in the light conversation. No need to take out her troubles on her friends.

There was a festive air about the dimly lit restaurant as she followed Joss and Louise to a center table. The muffled rhythmic beat of mariachis mingled with the sounds of hushed conversation and clinking china. Almost immediately a waiter arrived with a basket piled high with crisp, hot tortilla chips and a bowl of a peppery hot *picante* sauce.

Both Louise and Joss seemed to be deeply absorbed in scrutinizing the large selection on the menu. At length Joss signaled for the waiter and held a long discussion about the off-menu items. In the end he settled on the first entrée he had mentioned when they arrived.

171

Tiffany began to wonder why she had accepted this invitation. After all, Louise hadn't known Van was supposed to be calling her. What if her phone was ringing now?

Stop it, she ordered herself, smiling at the dark, round-cheeked waiter. "I'll have the *chili relleno,*" she told him.

"With or without the cheese sauce?" asked Joss.

"With the sauce, naturally," said Tiffany, bewildered by Joss's intent interest in the food tonight. "Isn't it always served with sauce?"

The waiter nodded, equally bewildered. "What type of chilies do you use in the *relleno?*" persisted Joss.

"*Poblano.* We do have others available if the señorita would prefer."

"No, I'll have the usual," snapped Tiffany with a darting look at Joss. What *was* his problem tonight?

"You know what we ought to do?" Joss said as the waiter moved away.

"What?" asked Louise.

"We ought to take a trip together. I think all of us have been working too hard. Where would you like to go?"

"Now?" She hadn't worked at Windsor Enterprises long enough to have earned a vacation.

"Just dream a little," prompted Louise.

"Oh, in that case," Tiffany smiled in anticipation, "I've always wanted to visit Hawaii. How about you?"

"Australia's my dream," said Joss.

"England for me," chimed in Louise. "I want to see the lake country, visit Beatrice Potter's cottage, walk down the lanes where all the poets once walked."

"Sounds like you've got this all planned," said Joss.

"Everything but packing my bags."

The desultory conversation continued as they munched on the chips and then were served creamy avocado salads on beds of shredded lettuce. Tiffany felt herself relaxing, thankful for good friends who cared enough to entertain her on what would have been a lonely, miserable evening. From the intimate glances passing between the two of them, Tiffany suspected that their friendship was deepening, perhaps gradually ripening into the kind of love that would lead to marriage.

That must have been the problem with her attraction to Van from the beginning. Hadn't he said more than once they could never be friends? His attention must have been based on physical attraction . . . her looks were a dead ringer for the type of woman he was known to prefer. What chance would a relationship have had for them, anyway? The thought was scarcely comforting, at best.

The arrival of their food brought her attention back to the present as she sliced through the tender green chili filled with cheese and wrapped in a golden brown batter. The creamy cheese sauce was speckled with spices and hot to the taste. At length, Tiffany leaned back.

"I've eaten entirely too much but that was absolutely delicious. Why haven't we tried this place before?"

"It's on our list from now on," agreed Louise.

"Anyone for dessert?" asked Joss.

"Not me." Tiffany rolled her eyes in mock distress, surprised by the sharp glance Joss shot Louise's way.

"Yes . . . dessert . . . of course," Louise stuttered, as if on cue.

"You almost never take dessert, Louise," Tiffany pointed out.

"Tonight's special."

"Special?"

"The mystery's been solved. All of us are in the clear," broke in Joss.

"Yes, you're right. I guess I haven't fully realized it yet," agreed Tiffany slowly. There were still too many unresolved mysteries in her personal life to feel much sense of relief.

Joss signaled once more for the waiter and began a maddeningly long discussion of the possibilities for dessert. When the waiter explained that the chef would prepare fresh pineapple *empanadas* if they would settle for a long wait, Joss agreed instantly. "Pineapple *empanadas*. Wonderful! We'll have that."

"Yes, pineapple *empanadas*," trilled Louise. "Just what my taste buds are watering for."

Tiffany's suspicions grew. She distinctly remembered Louise mentioning that she broke into hives when she ate fresh pineapple. Any doubt she'd had that they had been ordered to keep her out all evening vanished. Why? To prevent a repeat of her earlier call to Mrs. Duncan? Embarrassment, mingled with rising anger flooded her. Van didn't have any reason to feel responsible for her.

While they waited the waiter brought cups of the restaurant's special coffee and they leaned back, sipping slowly, listening to the mariachi band. Tiffany glanced over at the window and froze. Through the arched glass she could see the outline of several men. One reminded her of Van and she had to blink back tears, suddenly furious with herself for being so vulnerable at the sight of anyone faintly resembling him.

She stared down at the cup in her hand, trying to regain her composure. Lost in her own world, she gradually became aware that the usual noise in the restaurant had subsided and everyone seemed poised in a state of hushed expectancy.

Glancing up, she surprised a delighted grin on Joss's ruddy face before flicking a glance around the room. At the entrance to the dining room stood three men dressed in the costumes of Spanish troubadours. The first man carried a guitar over his shoulder and he was leading the others directly to their table.

When he reached the center of the room, he adjusted his guitar and announced loudly, "Ladies and gentlemen, we are here to serenade the lovely Señorita Martin."

Bowing deeply before Tiffany, all three men made a great show of surrounding her chair. From somewhere, the beam of a spotlight bathed Tiffany and the serenaders in a brilliant band of light. Tiffany was almost numb with surprise, allowing the blend of romantic lyrics and soft music to flow over and around her until she leaned back, closing her eyes, determined to enjoy this moment no matter what its source or meaning.

She felt a movement on the red leather banquette beside her and her eyes flew open, colliding with Van's dark gaze as he slipped his arm around her waist.

"Hello, darling," he murmured.

175

Colors and sounds and movements streaked together in a brilliant kaleidoscope. Time stood still. The world included only the two of them, nothing intruding on the beauty of the moment.

"Van, I . . . thought . . ." Sobs of pure joy choked back her words.

"I'm sorry I'm late," he murmured, his words difficult to hear above the lilting strains of the serenaders. "I wanted this evening to be so perfect for us."

The music stopped as abruptly as it had begun and Tiffany forced herself to join in the cheering applause as the serenaders moved off, wending their way to the center stage, guided by the beam of light.

"You two knew all along!" Tiffany accused Joss and Louise. She was melting into the warmth of Van's cradling arm, still not fully realizing what was happening to her.

"He said to keep you busy."

Van was laughing. "Was she giving you any trouble?"

"I couldn't have held out much longer," said Louise with a laugh. "When I pretended to like fresh pineapple . . ."

"You're going to eat every bite of them," said Tiffany in the most menacing tone she could manage. She was longing to be alone with Van. Why had he wanted this moment to be so public?

His hand stroked her bare arm, sending a shiver of excitement through her that heightened as he bent over and brushed a kiss on her flushed cheek. "I think we'll have to take Joss's word that Louise eats her share. That is, unless you're still hungry."

Tiffany eyed him teasingly. "And what will you say if I say I am?"

He groaned, "You wouldn't dare do that to me, Tiff. Will you two excuse us?" He nodded to Louise and Joss.

"With our blessings," said Louise. "I'm so happy about all of this, I may burst . . ."

"Hold off, Lou," said Joss gruffly. "Maybe you're jumping the gun a little."

"She's not even halfway keeping up," said Van, tugging Tiffany gently along behind him as he slid to the end of the bench. He grasped her arm and whisked her out of the restaurant and into his car, where an attendant stood holding the door open.

"You were very sure of yourself, weren't you?" said Tiffany lightly as he started the engine and pulled out into the traffic.

"I'm never certain of anything where you're concerned, Tiff. As soon as I can find a quiet place to pull over, we have some things to discuss."

Within minutes he had drawn the car smoothly to the curb on a residential street. After shutting off the engine, he sat looking at Tiffany for a few moments, his gaze moving over her face as if he were memorizing each delicate feature. Tiffany found it increasingly difficult to breathe, longing to trace the sensual curve of his lips, desperate to feel his arms around her, his mouth covering hers.

He broke the silence. "I love you, Tiffany. I have for a long time, but I've been fighting it."

The love and happiness that flooded her could be withheld no longer. She put her arms around his neck, tilting her head to look into his eyes. "Don't talk, Van. Please hold me before I die."

His arms encircled her with a swift fierceness, pressing into her back, and his mouth found hers, the kisses filled with passion and love and a barely restrained desperation to make her a part of him, never to let her go. When he lifted his head, he stopped in alarm. "You're crying. What's wrong?"

"I couldn't be crying. I've never been so happy." With a small gesture of embarrassment, she made a futile effort to scrub the tears off her cheeks.

Van captured her small hand in his, smiling tenderly. "Let me." Gently he kissed away the tears, murmuring words of love and endearment as he rocked her back and forth in his arms. "Never cry over me, darling. I'm not worth it."

"You're worth everything to me."

He leaned back. "One of those things money can't buy? I've learned a lot since I first met you, Tiffany. I understand now what you were trying to tell me."

"But I can't believe I had the nerve to say all those things to you. What am I going to do about my big mouth, Van?"

"May I help?" Bending down, he gave her a swift, hard kiss. "I want you to promise me something."

As if she had it within her power to refuse him. "What?"

"That you'll never hold back anything you want to tell me. I want our marriage to be built on trust and openness. I don't want either of us ever to have to wonder what the other is thinking."

Tiffany's eyes glittered as she pushed lightly against Van's chest. "Did I miss something?"

He appeared puzzled for only a moment and then began laughing. "Forgive me, darling. I'm asking you to marry me. Would you—could you find a way to put up with me?" His tone was suddenly that of a man utterly dependent on her next words.

"Yes! Yes! Yes!," said Tiffany, fighting back the warm tears flooding her eyes once more. "I love you, Van!"

With a swift intake of breath he gathered her once more against him. At last Van drew back and gazed at her, the searing look of pure love and tenderness so intense it made Tiffany catch her breath. "I love you," she repeated.

"Not half as much as I love you. Just think, my sweet one, we'll have a marriage based on so much more than I ever knew was possible. We'll have God's love blessing us, guiding us, giving us a way to understand each other. I have so much to learn about Him."

"We both do, darling. Will you be hurt if I tell you I had real doubt that you'd ever become a Christian?"

Van chuckled, that familiar sound that made her feel warm and content inside. "I can't blame you. Can you imagine what I would have said if anyone had told me a year ago I'd be reading the Bible as avidly as if it were a best seller?"

"It *is*. The world's *best* best seller for all ages."

"See?" He dropped a kiss on her nose. "You'll have to teach me."

"You've already learned to trust me." She snuggled against him. " I was so afraid you'd believe I had invited Bob Hartman to my apartment."

His look was one of pure amazement. "You? It never crossed my mind! One of the reasons I was late tonight was because I had a little talk with Bob's father. Mr. Hartman agreed that Bob needs to be transferred to Hong Kong for a couple of years until he grows up."

"I'm glad he's leaving town. How about Pam?" Reaching out to brush back a strand of the jet-black hair that had dropped over his forehead, Tiffany pleaded. "You *will* go easy on her, won't you, Van?"

"You soft-hearted little sweetheart," he teased. "What did you think? That I'd order her boiled in oil?"

"No, but she really doesn't have any family, and. . .well, I feel responsible for her."

"I've already talked to her. She's decided to work for a temporary agency while she goes to a training school for social secretaries."

Tiffany laughed knowingly. "A perfect place to meet rich men. Was she very happy that you weren't going to file charges against her?"

"I think so. And it gave me an opportunity to explain about my new faith in Christ."

"Van, I'm so proud of you!"

"Pam would never have listened if she hadn't already seen your example these last few months. You've brought about a lot of changes at Windsor Enterprises."

Tiffany flushed with pleasure, rubbing her cheek against his. "What are you trying to do? Give me a big head? It won't take you long to find out what a temper I have."

"I'm ready," he said, nuzzling the side of her neck with his lips. "Is there any reason why we can't marry soon?"

"I can't think of a one. . .that is, if my employer will give me some time off."

EPILOGUE

In the soft rays of November sunshine, the oak
trees shimmered and the leaves were beginning to fall,
spattering the lawns with crimson and bronze and
gold. The air, although cool, held only the hint of
autumn and the crowds making their way down the
path to the small white church, were comfortable in
lightweight clothing.

For days, the residents of Woodville, Texas, had
been hearing rumors about the wealthy and famous
who would be attending the wedding of Tiffany Martin
and Van Windsor. The church Tiffany had chosen for
the ceremony was over a hundred years old, a white
wooden structure nestled among tall pines and stately
oaks on the edge of town. Her family had been
members here for several generations, but now she
alone was left. Having her wedding in this historic
setting gave her a warm feeling of continuity and
closeness to those she missed so keenly. It did present
a problem, though. The church sanctuary was small,

and only a few select guests could attend the actual ceremony.

Many of Tiffany's friends had gathered on folding chairs placed on the freshly trimmed church grounds to watch the arrival of the noteworthy guests.

Tiffany Martin was a favorite citizen of Woodville. Her mother and stepfather had been missed since their deaths, and, later, friends had mourned with Tiffany over the loss of her stepbrother, Barry. Returning here to marry one of Houston's most eligible young bachelors was in some ways a tribute to the memory of her loved ones.

A long procession of luxurious cars began arriving, discharging the distinguished guests, some of whom were recognizable from television or newspaper articles. The appearance of an antique silver-and-maroon Rolls Royce evoked a hushed silence. When it pulled to a stop, a uniformed chauffeur alighted and opened a rear door. The elderly woman accepting his assistance was gowned in peony silk taffeta with an opalescent sequined bodice and a bow-sashed waist. "The groom's grandmother," whispered one guest behind her hand. "I saw a newspaper photo of her cutting the ribbons for the opening of a hospital in Houston last week."

After several more minutes a sleek limousine drew to a halt in front of the church. The spectators strained to catch a glimpse of Tiffany as she emerged, but a stocky, ruddy-faced man temporarily obscured their view. Tiffany was resting her hand lightly on his arm. "Joss Collins," offered the same woman who had made the earlier announcement. "He's Van Windsor's assistant."

The majority of onlookers ignored the woman's

comments, their attention focused on Tiffany. To the accompaniment of little gasps and whispers of admiration, they watched as she flipped back a candlelight Brussel's lace veil, an heirloom of the Windsor family. It was worn mantilla-style and cascaded softly over the Alencon lace and ivory satin gown down to the magnificent train draped over Tiffany's free arm. She started down the pine needle-strewn path.

Suddenly aware of several close friends, Tiffany gave a quick wave and smile. "I think I'm being compared to Cinderella," she murmured to Joss.

Grinning, he patted her hand. "What does that make me? The fairy godmother?"

"Hardly," she laughed softly. "I'd say that was Louise's role. She kept reminding me what a great guy Van was even when I refused to believe a word of it."

Everything *had* worked out so marvelously, Tiffany mused. All the leaks in the company had stopped, and even Pam seemed to have learned a valuable lesson. Tiffany hoped she was here today. Pam needed to see for herself that God answers prayer—especially in the area of love and marriage. Given time. . . .

"If I remember correctly, Tiff, we all gave you a rough time," Joss said softly. "How're you doing now? Any bridal jitters?"

A quick glance at Joss revealed that he was the one having an attack of nerves. She squeezed his arm, giving him a reassuring smile.

The traditional strains of the wedding march sounded, and Tiffany started forward on Joss's arm, her long veil billowing behind her. The tinted rays of sunlight filtering through the stained-glass windows mesmerized her for a moment and then her eyes sought Van. He was standing at the altar, magnificent in his dark tuxedo, the frilly white shirt front accentuating his aristocratic tanned features. A slight smile slanted the curve of his lips as their eyes locked.

The miracle of it all struck Tiffany as she continued down the aisle, completely oblivious to the presence of anyone else in the church. Less than a year before, she'd met Van, never dreaming this moment would come for them. At first their differences had seemed insurmountable—her deep, abiding faith clashing with his cynicism; her small-town background paling in the bright lights of the international jet set scene. It shamed her to remember the times when she'd wondered why everything seemed to be going wrong in her life. Surely after this proof of God's loving faithfulness, she'd remember to trust Him in the future!

Van was standing completely still, his eyes focused on his bride, bathed in the rays of sunlight streaming through the windows. Not even her detailed description of the satin gown that had belonged to her mother, had prepared him for the vision approaching him. The folds of the gown shimmered as she moved, lending soft glow to her ivory skin. Her brown eyes were solemn as they steadfastly watched him, and the wonder of this moment swept over him as she reached his side, and he held out his hand to support her last few steps to the altar.

With Joss beside him and Louise standing next to Tiffany, the ceremony began. Tiffany gazed up at Van, and his heart contracted. She had never seemed so irresistible! It hardly seemed possible that he was getting married. He, Van Windsor, who had scoffed at the very idea of marriage! But that was before he had met Tiffany and before he had learned about the Divine love that had the power to transform even the most skeptical of men!

The ceremony was a traditional one, chosen by Van when Tiffany's minister had mentioned the options open to them. The words were achingly beautiful . . . "Dearly beloved, we are gathered together today in the presence of God and these witnesses . . . To love, to honor, to cherish . . . For better or for worse . . . for richer, for poorer . . . in sickness and in health . . . Till death do us part." *Yes, that's what I want,* Van thought. *Nothing short of total commitment could ever satisfy the love I have for this woman.*

He took her left hand in his and slipped the ring over her slender finger—the ring that had been given by his father to his mother on another wedding day. Tiffany had preferred it to the much more expensive ones he'd offered her. Precious Tiffany—so infinitely precious. He saw the tears glistening on her long lashes as she gazed into his eyes, and he knew he had never loved her more than he did at that moment.

Eyes as soft and warm as a fawn's smiled up at him. Van touched a tendril of fair hair that had escaped from the confinement of her veil, and he outlined the contour of her face with the tip of his finger before bending to kiss her softly, tenderly, reverently. With her, his heart was safe—for the rest of their lives.

ABOUT THE AUTHORS

ELAINE ANNE McAVOY is the pseudonym for a prolific mother-daughter writing team, separated by a distance of more than a thousand miles. Though our high-tech society has provided them sophisticated tools of their trade via computer, they confess to keeping the U.S. Postal Service and AT&T quite busy as well.

Both ladies travel extensively, absorbing cultures and lifestyles that have contributed to their writing careers. Undergirding all their activities is a strong and abiding faith that finds expression in their books. *Irresistible Love* is their first Serenade/Serenata.

A Letter To Our Readers

Dear Reader:

Pioneering is an exhilarating experience, filled with opportunities for exploring new frontiers. The Zondervan Corporation is proud to be the first major publisher to launch a series of inspirational romances designed to inspire and uplift as well as to provide wholesome entertainment. In order that we might better contribute to your reading enjoyment, we would appreciate your taking a few minutes to respond to the following questions and return to:

Anne Severance, Editor
Serenade/Serenata Books
Zondervan Publishing House
1415 Lake Drive, S.E.
Grand Rapids, Michigan 49506

1. Did you enjoy reading IRRESISTIBLE LOVE?
   ☐ Very much. I would like to see more books by this author!
   ☐ Moderately
   ☐ I would have enjoyed it more if _____

2. Where did you purchase this book? _____

3. What influenced your decision to purchase this book?
   ☐ Cover   ☐ Back cover copy
   ☐ Title   ☐ Friends
   ☐ Publicity   ☐ Other _____

4. Please rate the following elements from 1 (poor) to 10 (superior):

☐ Heroine ☐ Plot
☐ Hero ☐ Inspirational theme
☐ Setting ☐ Secondary characters

5. Which settings would you like to see in future Serenade/Serenata Books?

_____   _____

_____   _____

6. What are some inspirational themes you would like to see treated in future Serenade books?

_____   _____

_____   _____

7. Would you be interested in reading other Serenade/Serenata or Serenade/Saga Books?

☐ Very interested
☐ Moderately interested
☐ Not interested

8. Please indicate your age range:

☐ Under 18 ☐ 25–34 ☐ 46–55
☐ 18–24 ☐ 35–45 ☐ Over 55

9. Would you be interested in a Serenade book club? If so, please give us your name and address:

Name _____

Occupation _____

Address _____

City _____ State _____ Zip _____

Serenade/Serenata Books are inspirational romances in contemporary settings, designed to bring you a joyful, heart-lifting reading experience.

Serenade/Serenata books now available in your local bookstore:

#1   ON WINGS OF LOVE, Elaine L. Schulte
#2   LOVE'S SWEET PROMISE,
      Susan C. Feldhake
#3   FOR LOVE ALONE, Susan C. Feldhake
#4   LOVE'S LATE SPRING, Lydia Heermann
#5   IN COMES LOVE, Mab Graff Hoover
#6   FOUNTAIN OF LOVE, Velma S. Daniels
      and Peggy E. King
#7   MORNING SONG, Linda Herring
#8   A MOUNTAIN TO STAND STRONG,
      Peggy Darty
#9   LOVE'S PERFECT IMAGE, Judy Baer
#10   SMOKY MOUNTAIN SUNRISE,
      Yvonne Lehman
#11   GREENGOLD AUTUMN,
      Donna Fletcher Crow

Watch for these Serenade Books in the coming months:

      WINTERSPRING, Sandy Dengler
      (Serenade/Saga #12)
      ETERNAL FLAME, Lurlene McDaniel
      (Serenade/Serenata #13)